Ada Yardeni

A-dventure-Z'

The Story of the Alphabet

Ada Yardeni

A-dventure-Z'

The Story of the Alphabet

Revised and expanded from the original Hebrew edition
HARPATKA'OT © 1983, 1993

ISBN 956-220-531-1

Contents

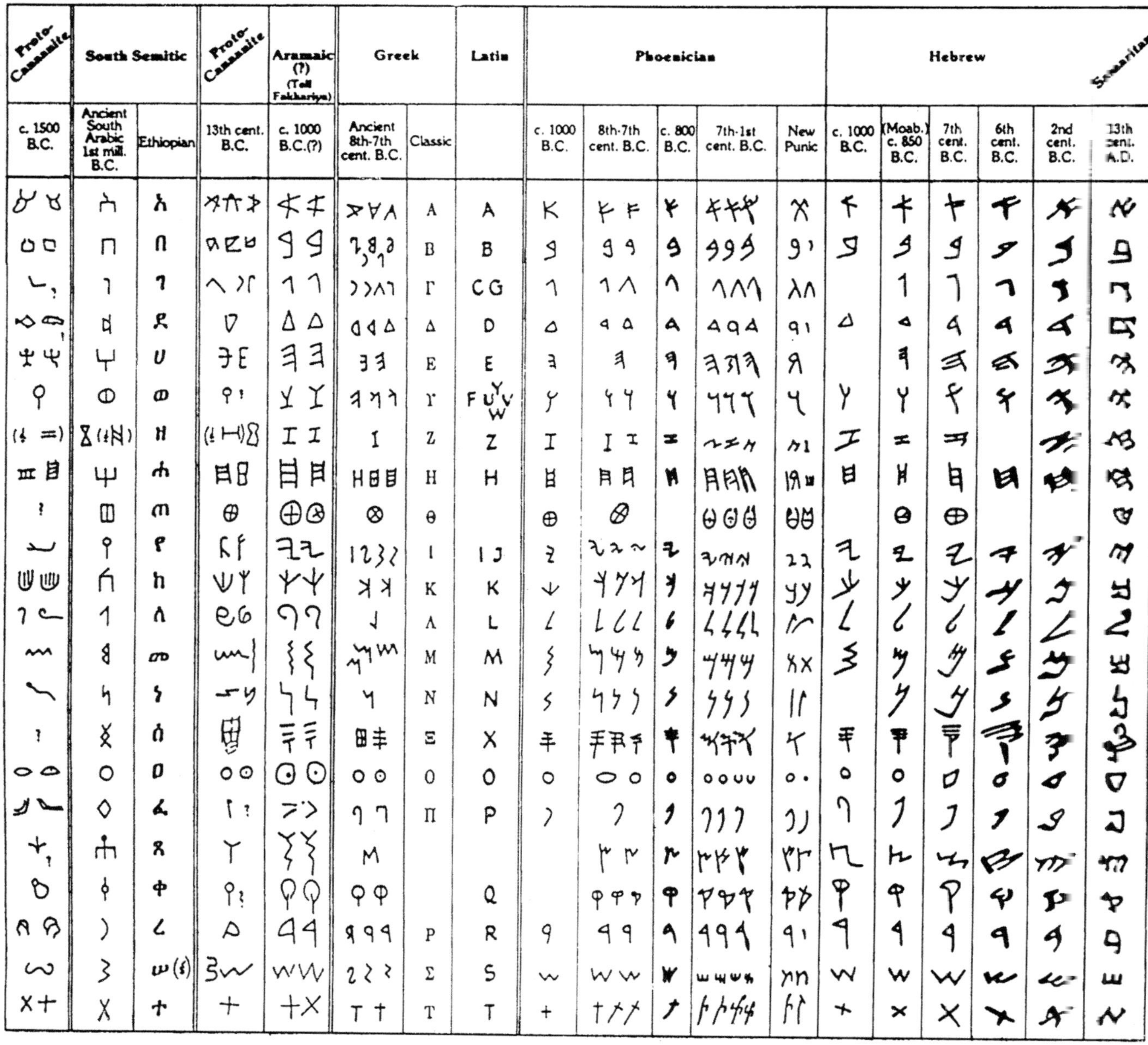
Proto-Canaanite
South Semitic
Proto-Canaanite
Aramaic (?) (Tell Fakhariya)
Greek
Latin
Phoenician
Hebrew
Samaritan
c. 1500 B.C.
Ancient South Arabic 1st mill. B.C.
Ethiopian
13th cent. B.C.
c. 1000 B.C.(?)
Ancient 8th-7th cent. B.C.
Classic
c. 1000 B.C.
8th-7th cent. B.C.
c. 800 B.C.
7th-1st cent. B.C.
New Punic
c. 1000 B.C.
(Moab.) c. 850 B.C.
7th cent. B.C.
6th cent. B.C.
2nd cent. B.C.
13th cent. A.D.

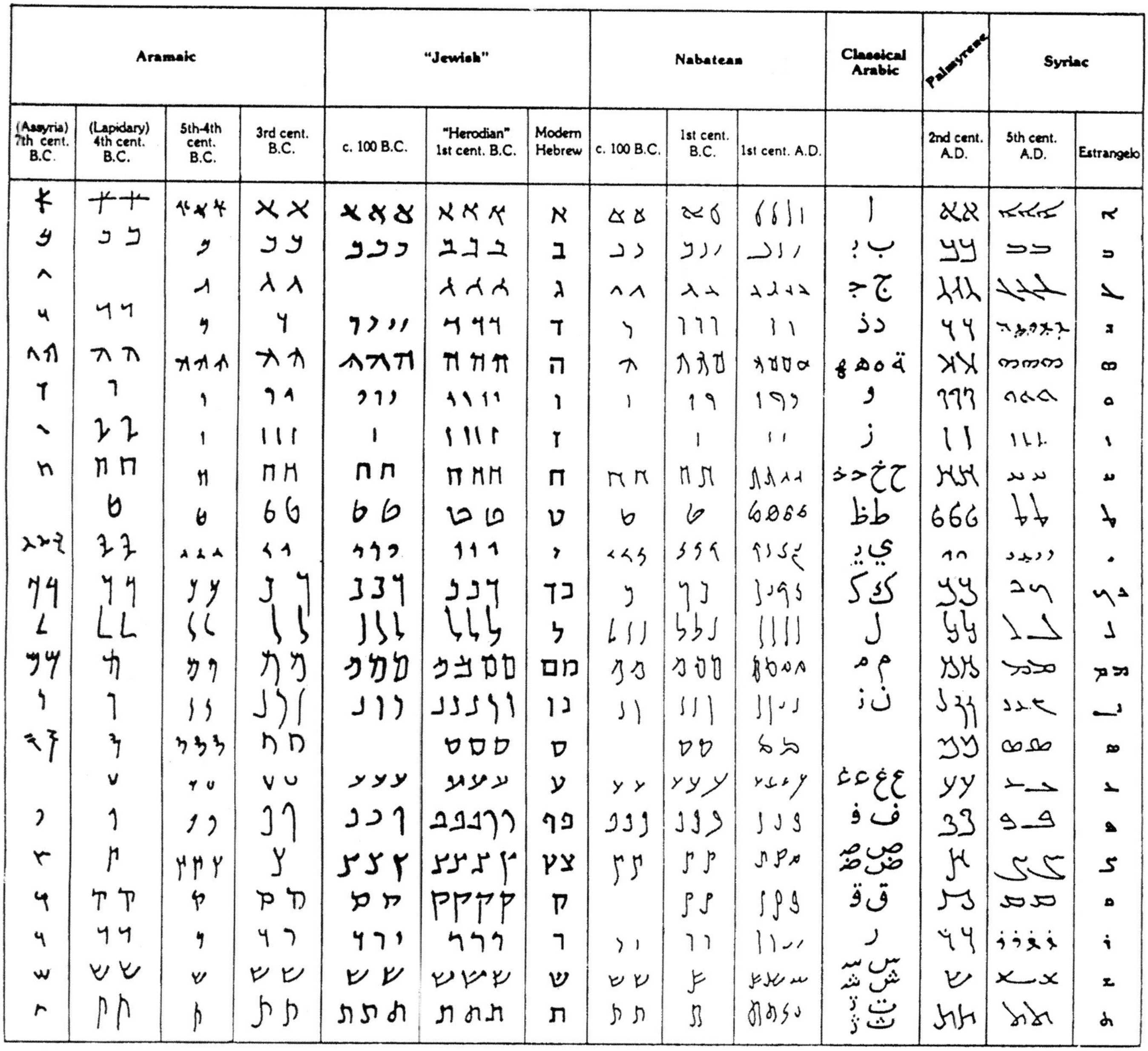
Aramaic
"Jewish"
Nabatean
Classical Arabic
Palmyrene
Syriac
(Assyria) 7th cent. B.C.
(Lapidary) 4th cent. B.C.
5th-4th cent. B.C.
3rd cent. B.C.
c. 100 B.C.
"Herodian" 1st cent. B.C.
Modern Hebrew
c. 100 B.C.
1st cent. B.C.
1st cent. A.D.
2nd cent. A.D.
5th cent. A.D.
Estrangelo
א
ב
ג
ד
ה
ו
ז
ח
ט
י
כך
ל
מם
נן
ס
ע
פף
צץ
ק
ר
ש
ת

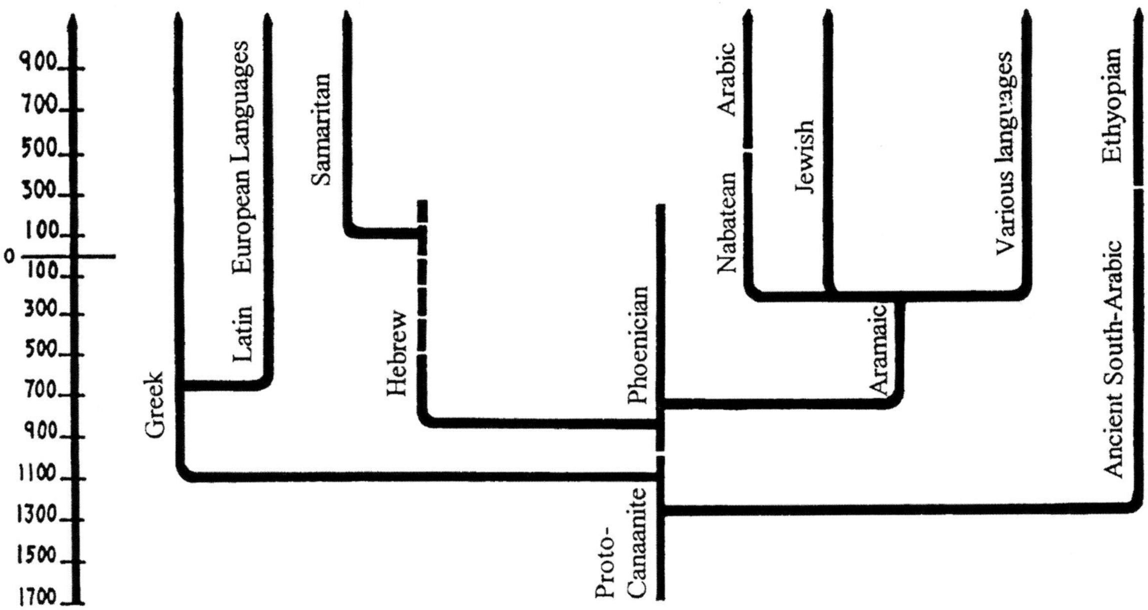
900
700
500
300
100
0
100
300
500
700
900
1100
1300
1500
1700
Greek
Latin
European Languages
Samaritan
Hebrew
Proto-Canaanite
Phoenician
Aramaic
Nabatean
Arabic
Jewish
Various languages
Ancient South-Arabic
Ethyopian

Introduction

Before loudspeakers were invented, people could not converse with each other from a distance greater than that carried by the human voice. The search for an efficient method of communication was one of the factors in the invention of the script. We still are amazed at this wonderful invention, which has been one of the basic factors in the development of human culture, and its faithful servant for thousands of years.

Various writing systems evolved through the ages in different places, and there are languages which until a short while ago used thousands of script-signs for their writing. The alphabetic system, which contains a relative small number of signs, is one of the most efficient writing systems and was gradually adopted for the writing of many languages. It serves most of the nations in the world, except for the large group in the Far East and certain small groups in remote places.

Although it constitutes a single system, the alphabet has had many different manifestations, perhaps due to the use of different writing materials and implements in various times and places. The linear alphabetic scripts evolved from a pictographic script of approximately 30 signs. In the course of time, the forms of the signs changed and many different forms emerged, but the connections between these forms became unrecognizable.

The tracing of the consecutive phases in this formal evolution, from the common ancient signs to their forms in the different scripts, is possible thanks to the large number of ancient inscriptions and manuscripts discovered in the last two centuries, when archaeology became a recognized science. Palaeography and epigraphy became the basis for the decipherment and interpretation of ancient writings. A number of scholars in various countries devoted their time and energy to the study of the ancient languages and scripts in order to reveal the secrets of these ancient writings to the modern world.

The study of the letter-forms can be a real entertainment when we understand the logic of their formal development, i.e., the natural connection between a certain form and the immediately preceding and succeeding forms. Deciphering inscriptions in ancient scripts can be a thrilling experience resembling the cracking of a secret code. The examination of the formal changes which occurred in the alphabetic signs is an experience which may also be compared to listening to a musical work and enjoying the elaborations and variations on a theme.

The resemblance between the Hebrew and Arabic languages is observable in their lexicography and grammar, but it is quite difficult to recognize a similarity in the forms of the letters in the Arabic, Hebrew and Latin scripts. However, if we examine the changes which occurred in the letter-forms of the alphabet, it will be easier for us to discover the links between them.

Hebrew and Arabic, belonging to the 'Semitic' family of languages, differ in lexicography and grammar from the languages of other families, including the 'Indo-European' family. Nevertheless, the alphabetic letter-signs are used in the writing of the languages of these two families, although the resemblance between the letter-signs of the different alphabetic scripts can hardly be discerned.

In this book, we will reveal the secrets of the common origin of the alphabetic letter-forms and trace their evolution in various scripts.

***

In the beginning, people were ignorant of writing.

Instead of writing they drew on rocks or stones. But they drew only what they saw and could not draw their thoughts.
For example, they could draw  a foot,  a hand,  an eye,  a head,  a house,  a snake and all that is concrete.
But they could not draw the words 'I love you', or 'The weather is fine', or people's names like Jonathan or Hagith.
This was the situation until the alphabet was born.
The alphabet was not invented in a single day; the time and the place of its invention are unknown. However, on the basis of ancient inscriptions that have been discovered, scholars have reconstructed the phases in the evolution of the letters.

The following tale is meant to illustrate the miracle of the invention of the alphabet.

***

Tale

Once upon a time, there was a great and noble king in the land of Canaan. The king loved to sing. Every morning, after rising from his large, golden bed, he would take his golden harp and sing of the trees and the sun, the flowing stream and the eyes of the beautiful maiden he loved. The songs were so beautiful that they captured everyone's heart and the rhymes and verses made magical sounds. Each day the king composed new verses and the birds accompanied his singing with their chirpings. The people were enchanted by the beauty of the songs and praised their talented king.

Then a thought crossed the king's mind: "What a pity that my songs are forgotten. If only I could preserve the songs so that I could sing them over and over again, and other people could sing my songs as well." The king became very unhappy and his songs were sadder and sadder.

The people in the court wondered what had happened to their beloved king and wanted to console him. So they sent to the king the wisest and oldest counsellor to discover the reason for the king's unhappiness.
And this is what the king told the counsellor: "The reason for my sorrow is that my beautiful songs perish and pass into oblivion and I know of no way to preserve them."
To this the counsellor replied:
"Let the king send posts all over the country to find a wise person who could help our Majesty the King in this matter."

Following the king's order, messengers went out in haste and ran towards the borders of the kingdom. When they reached the border of Egypt, the residents told them that in Egypt there were skilled people who knew how to draw poems and stories. The messengers hurried back to tell the king the wonderful news. On hearing this, the king ordered a messenger to be sent immediately to Egypt to acquire the skills of drawing poems and stories.

On arriving in Egypt, the messenger was brought to the king's court and shown the king's scribe sitting on the ground and drawing various pictures with a reed pen on a papyrus scroll stretched out on his skirt.
The messenger sat down near the scribe and watched him drawing the pictures, trying to understand their meanings. Then the scribe said to the messenger:
"The work of the scribe is an ancient profession, as ancient as the sphinx. It is a difficult and exalted craft, and only a few people are capable of acquiring the skills of a professional scribe."

To his amazement, the messenger learned that the pictures told long and wonderful tales and each picture described not only objects one can see but also thoughts and feelings.
Then the messenger said to himself:
"Now I have learned something excellent. I'll come to my king and tell him thus: 'Let the king draw a picture of a sun when he wants to draw the words 'heat', 'light', 'day', or an eye when he wants to draw the idea 'to see', or a foot when he wants to draw the words 'to go', and in that way he will be able to draw his poems and his thoughts'."

The messenger hurried back to the land of Canaan to bring the good news to the king.

The king was thrilled with joy hearing the messenger's news and appointed him to be his scribe.

The next morning the king awoke from his sleep happy and enthusiastic; he took his harp and started to sing while the scribe sat at his feet ready to begin his work.
And this was the song the king sang:

> "The loveliness of your beauty is a song that is sung,
> making all hearts rejoice.
> How pleasant are you in my eyes, O graceful maiden!"

And in his language it sounded as follows:

> *No^{c}am yoffiekh zemer mitnagen, marnyn kol lev.*
> *Ma na^{c}amt li bat khen.*

The scribe dipped his reed pen into the ink and tried to draw the Canaanite word for loveliness, but he had completely forgotten how one draws the word *No^{c}am*. In the meantime the king continued to sing and the scribe sat with the reed pen in his hand, bending his head in sorrow and shame.
The king saw the misery of the scribe, and his song died away and the gleam faded from his eyes.

The scribe confessed to the king that he was unable to remember how to draw the word *No^{c}am*.

The king was very sad and disappointed; the following night he could not sleep, troubled by his thoughts and uncertain what to do.

The next morning he gathered the council of elders and ordered them to put their heads together to solve the question of how the scribe could draw all the words.

The council met for a hundred days and a hundred nights, endeavouring to find an answer to the question, and at the end of that time they arrived at a very important decision. And since the problem was so difficult to solve, the solution they reached was extremely sophisticated and somewhat complicated, but wonderful like the solution to some very complicated riddle. And this is what they decided:

"When the scribe wants to draw the first sound in the word *No*^{c}*am*, he should draw the creature which is called *nun* in the Canaanite language , since both words begin with the same sound, /*n*/. Then he should draw an eye called ^{c}*ayin* in Canaanite  , since it begins with the sound that appears next in the word *No*^{c}*am*. Then only one sound will be left, and that is the sound /*m*/. The scribe should draw water  which is *maym* in Canaanite and which begins with the sound /*m*/, and thus he will have three pictures which together form the main sounds of the word *No*^{c}*am* since this word has no picture of its own."

"In the same way he will draw a hand , which in Canaanite is *yad*, and a mouth  , which in Canaanite is *pe*, and other pictures of various objects, combining the first sounds of their names to form all the words appearing in the song which have no pictures of their own and which represent thoughts and ideas."

Then the members of the council chose a number of pictures, discovering to their amazement that they needed less than thirty pictures for the composition of all the words in the Canaanite language.

They immediately sent a messenger to the king to announce this wonderful and thrilling discovery.

The king was very astonished and said:
"In this way, every person will be able to learn how to write, since it is not difficult to recognize a relatively small number of pictures and to learn by heart the sounds which they represent; and if all the people will be familiar with these pictures they will be able to read my beautiful songs."

The king was so happy that he immediately ordered a large and magnificent banquet for all his court, and he proudly presented to all the song written in large, beautiful pictures :

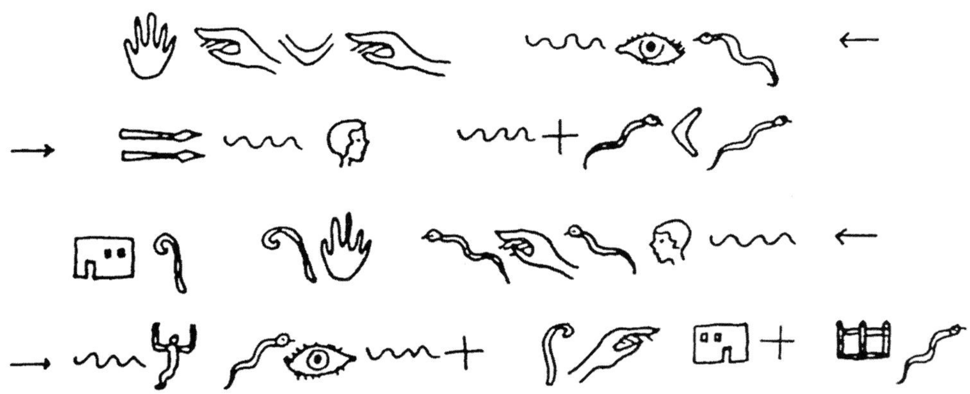

***

The Alphabet

In ancient times people did not speak Hebrew or Arabic or English or French, because these languages have not yet come into being. But their ancestors and relatives which resembled them, though not precisely, already existed. In the land of Canaan, for example, people spoke the Canaanite language. In this language, the word for 'head' was *ra'sh* and the word for 'water' was *may* or *maym*. An ox was called *alluf* or *alf*, a house was called *bayt* and a kind of boomerang was called *gaml*.
These Canaanite words, with slight variations, have survived in the names of our letters, but this happened so long ago that today we no longer remember the meaning of all the words. Thus, for example, we do not remember the meaning of the word *Tet* but only the form preserved in the letter-sign.

When people realized that they could draw all the words, they began drawing all the things they wished to remember. But this was a long procedure, because it is difficult and tiring to draw a house or an eye or the head of an ox again and again. They therefore decided to draw only the main lines of the pictures. For example:  *alf* ,  *bayt*, etc.

In this way they could, for example, write the word *ab* meaning 'father' or the word *kalb* meaning 'dog':

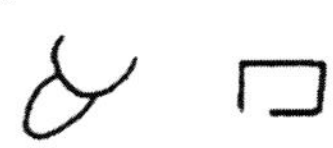

But, even so, the writing took a long time, because people wanted to write many things, such as stories or letters to each other, and sometimes they were in a hurry and wanted to send a quick note to someone. And then a strange thing happened to the pictures - their forms began to change. This happened because, when written rapidly and spontaneously the letter-forms change; sometimes a stroke moves or gets separated from another stroke; sometimes a stroke becomes longer or shorter or even disappears, and sometimes it makes a curve and joins the following stroke. Thus many changes occurred in the pictures, and various forms of the same sign were created from one picture.

The most ancient inscriptions in the early alphabetic pictographic script date from about the 19th century BCE and were discovered in Egypt. Inscriptions in a similar script, apparently dating one or two centuries later, were discovered in the Sinai peninsula. This script apparently contained 28 or 29 pictographic signs, corresponding to the number of consonants in the proto-Canaanite language, the language which gave birth to the Canaanite languages. In approximately the 13th century BCE, the western Canaanite dialects contained a smaller number of consonants than the Proto-Canaanite mother-language, and accordingly the number of signs for writing these dialects was reduced to 22. The descendants of the Canaanites, the residents of Tyre and Sidon, who are called Phoenicians, used these same 22 signs, which had already become stylized, linear letters, and wrote them exclusively in horizontal lines from right to left.

The Greeks probably adopted the Canaanite alphabet in about 1100 BCE, but the earliest inscriptions in their alphabet, still written from right to left, date from about 800 BCE; in the course of time the direction of writing changed and consequently the positions and forms of the letters. The Romans received the alphabetic script from the Greeks via the Etruscans and transmitted their version, known as the Latin script, to most European nations.

Other peoples who inherited the Phoenician script were the Israelites and later the Aramaeans. The ancient Hebrew script, commonly known as *Da^{c}ats* or *Ra^{c}ats*, evolved from the Phoenician script in about the 9th century BCE, while the Aramaic script broke away from its Phoenician mother script in about the 8th century BCE.

When the Aramaic language prevailed in the vast Persian empire, extdnding from India to Ethiopia, in the 5th-3rd centuries BCE, the Aramaic script was used throughout this empire and the various nations wrote their languages in this script. Among these nations were the Nabataeans and the Jews (who rejected their ancient script in favour of the new one, occasionally using the former in periods of national revival and for sacred scriptures). In about the 3rd century BCE, when the Persian empire was conquered by the Macedonian ruler Alexander the Great, the Aramaic language and script gradually divided into local dialects and scripts. The script known as the "Jewish script" has changed only slightly since then, while the Nabataean script developed a very cursive form from which the Arabic script evolved. The earliest inscriptions in the Arabic script are from the 6th century CE but certain inscriptions dating from the 4th century already show the early phases of its evolution.

The Latin script, as well as the Hebrew and Arabic, emerged a long time after the letters of the Canaanite alphabet came into being. Therefore, when these letters began to be used for the writing of these languages their forms were already very different from the early pictures. This is the reason for our difficulty in recognizing the common origin of these scripts and their relation to the Canaanite pictures. But by tracing the various phases in the evolution of the letter-forms we may clearly see the connection between the forms.

ا *ʾAlif*

A

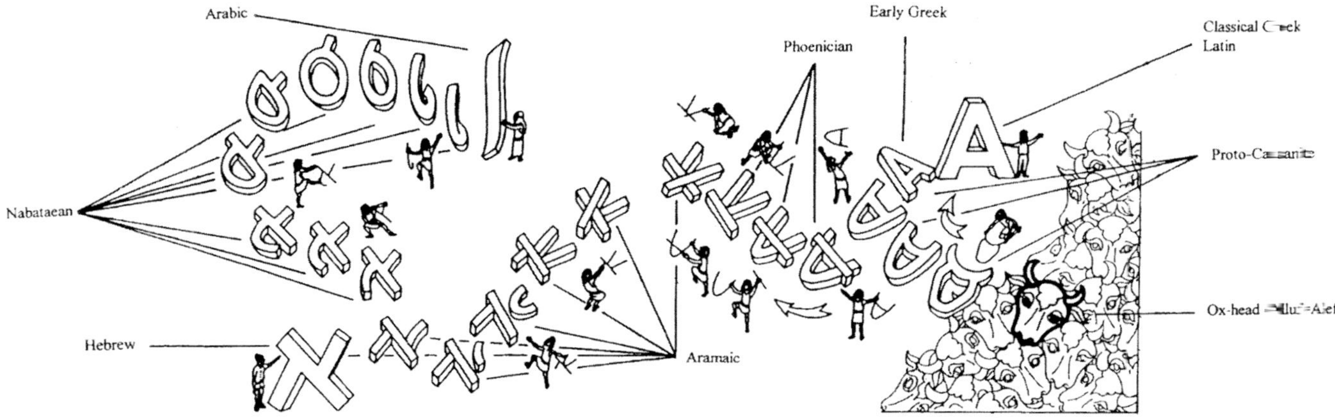

א *ʾAlef*

The first letter of the alphabet originated with the early Canaanite pictographic script, and its earliest form was a horned **ox-head** (Biblical Hebrew *ʾalluf*). Together with the other letters, it wandered with the Phoenician ships around the coasts of the Mediterranean, finding a home in ancient Greece, in the houses of its scholars and poets. The wanderings and vicissitudes of the journey changed its form until it became a triangle with two "legs" A. Since then, its form has changed very little. The Romans adopted it for the writing of their language and passed it on to other people as part of the Latin script. These people added various embellishments but retained its basic form. Its name and its phonetic expression vary accordingly to the different languages using the Latin script.

In Hebrew it is called Alef, and its modern form originated with the Aramaic script of the 5th century BCE. The family to which the Aramaic script belonged was a very venerable one, with roots somewhere in northern Syria around the end of the 2nd millennium BCE. Since the Aramaic script, like the ancient Hebrew script, is a descendant of the Canaanite script in its Phoenician transfiguration, the form of the Aramaic Alef can be traced back to the ox-head pictogram. In the course of time, the Alef sign changed its form and its lines separated and rejoined one another in different combinations. Eventually three main lines remained: א a diagonal, slanting downwards from left to right, and two shorter lines joining on both its sides. This was the basic form of the Aramaic Alef in about the 5th century BCE, when the Jews began to use the Aramaic script for their writings when residents of the Persian Empire. The "Jewish" script retained the basic form of this Aramaic Alef, which has been in use until this very day.

In Arabic, the letter is called Alif and its form is a long downstroke ا . The Arabic script evolved from the Nabataean script in about the 6th century CE, after a process lasting several centuries. The Nabataeans appear to have been one of the Arab tribes. They established a prosperous kingdom in the region surrounding the Dead Sea. Their kingdom existed during the first centuries BCE and until 106 CE, when it was conquered by the Romans and made into a Roman province called Provincia Arabia. The Nabataean script, like the "Jewish" script, evolved from the Aramaic script after the fall of the Persian empire in the late 4th century BCE. The Nabataeans developed a very cursive style of writing in which the letters tended to join each other. In a very short time they changed the form of the Aramaic letters; straight lines became curved and connected to each other. The diagonal and the left stroke of Alef drew towards each other, a process which had already begun in the Aramaic script in the 4th century BCE, creating the typical loop of the Nabataean Alef  , with a short stroke in a downwards direction on its upper right side.

This loop gradually became narrower  , and eventually became a simple downstroke. This was the form of early Arabic Alif. In the Arabic script, Alif joins to the right but does not join to the letter immediately following on the left. Its pronunciation resembles that of the Hebrew Alef: i.e., phonetically it is a guttural stop, but it also serves to designate the long vowel */a:/*.

ب *Ba:'*

B

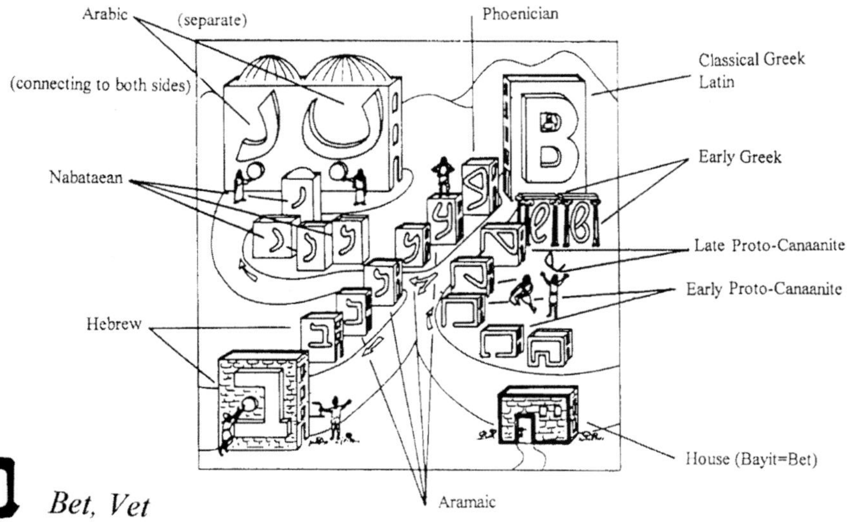

בּ,ב *Bet, Vet*

The Hebrew Bet ב , the Latin B and the Arabic Ba:' ب are the descendants of the ancient Canaanite sign which appears to have depicted a **house** (Hebrew *bayit*, Arabic *bayt*). In the languages using the Latin script, the name of the letter varies from language to language, but all begin with the consonant */b/*. When the Greeks inherited the script from the Canaanites, the Canaanite letter was made up of four lines , three lines constituting a triangle and a fourth line being drawn at a right angle beyond one of the angular points.

This was the form of the letter in about the 12th century BCE. In that period, the positions of the letter-signs were not fixed and their directions varied. The Phoenicians fixed the direction of writing in about the 11th century BCE. The ancient Greeks used various forms of the letter. When the Romans received the alphabet from the Greeks via the Etruscans, they chose only one of these forms. The letter B retained the same form in the Latin script as in the Greek, which was not the case with all the letters of the alphabet.

In Hebrew the letter is called Bet and the origin of the name seems to be the Canaanite word *bayt*, meaning 'house'. When the Aramaeans inherited the letters of the alphabet from the Phoenicians, the direction of writing had already been fixed. At that time the form of Bet was a triangle with its vertex pointing to the left, and its right stroke bending leftwards at the bottom 𐤁 . In the Aramaic script the top of the triangle opened up in the course of time 𐡁 .

In documents written in the "Jewish" script, dating from the 3rd century BCE onwards, Bet is written with three strokes, resembling a square ב open on its left side. In the course of time, the base-stroke of the "Jewish" Bet extended beyond its meeting point with the downstroke, creating a small protrusion on the lower right hand side ב. In Hebrew, Bet is sometimes written with a point inside the letter (called dagesh), indicating that the consonant should be pronounced /b/, whereas it is pronounced /v/ when written without this point.

In Arabic, the letter, originating in the Nabataean cursive script, is called Ba:'. When written in the middle of a word, its form sometimes resembled a comma ٮ . The same process occurred with a number of letters in the Nabataean cursive script, the forms of the letters deteriorating as a result of spontaneous or rapid writing until they became virtually identical to each other. In this way, the forms of Bet, Yod, Nun and Taw became identical when written in the middle of a word. In order to distinguish them from one another, in approximately the 8th century CE, diacritical points were added above or below these letters in the Arabic script. These diacritical points became an integral part of the letters in Arabic: بـ (Ba:'), تـ (Ta:'), نـ (Nu:n), يـ (Ya:').

Already in Nabataean inscriptions, many of the letters appear connected to each other, but not in accordance with a fixed system. In the Arabic script there are fixed rules for joining the letters. Some of the letters join only the immediately preceding letters, while others also join the immediately following ones. For example, the letter Ba:' joins on both sides; when preceding a letter which does not join to the right, Ba:' is larger and is drawn as a large concave curve ب. This is also its form at the end of words. Unlike the Hebrew Bet, which may be pronounced either as /b/ or as /v/, the Arabic Ba:' is only pronounced as /b/ (modern Arabic uses a Ba:' with three diacritical points to mark the consonant /p/, which does not exist in the Arabic language).

C,G

ج *Ji:m*

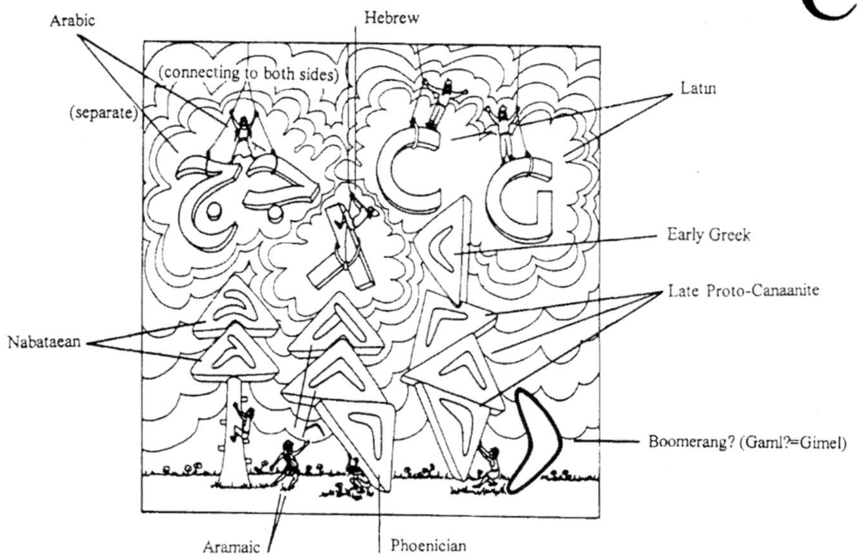

ג *Gimel*

The original form of the third letter of the alphabet is unknown. There are scholars who claim that Gimel was derived from the picture of an implement used as a **boomerang**, called *gaml* (Akkadian *gamlū*); other scholars relate it to the form of the **camel's hump**. In that case, the name Gimel would reflect that of the animal (Hebrew *gamal*). Certain scholars have interpreted as Gimel one of the signs appearing in the inscriptions discovered at Ṣerabit el-Khadim in the Sinai peninsula, but not all scholars agree that this sign, shaped like an angle ^, should be interpreted as Gimel. In later inscriptions, written in scripts originating in the Proto-Canaanite script, the letter does indeed have the shape of an angle 〉Γ. This form also appears in early Greek inscriptions. Variant forms of it appear in different places where the Greek script was used; the eastern Greek alphabet retained the two-stroke form Γ, and this is the form of the letter in the classical Greek script. The Romans, who adopted the western version of the Greek alphabet, preferred the curved form C, but they used it to designate the sound /s/.

In the languages using the Latin script, the letter C is called different names and designates various sounds. The same applies to the letter G, which was created by the addition of a small stroke to the C and which designates the sound */g/*.

In the Aramaic alphabet the sign changed only a little. The Phoenicians fixed its direction, facing leftwards 𐤂 . In the course of time, it tended to incline forwards in the direction of writing ∧ . In the Aramaic script, the left stroke slowly slipped down the right stroke 𐡂 , gradually reaching its centre, and it also appears in this form in the "Jewish" script.

In the region of Egypt and the Land of Israel, a reed pen and carbon-ink were used for writing on papyrus and on shards. In the course of time, the fluent writing on soft materials influenced the shape of the letters, and cursive script styles evolved. Due to a constant mutual influence, the cursive forms of the letters gradually found their way into the lapidary script, used on hard materials, and vice versa.

In the Nabataean cursive script, in which the letter-forms changed until scarcely recognizable, the left stroke of Gimel continued to slip down the right stroke until it reached its bottom 𐢃 , and in addition, both strokes curved and the form of Gimel became identical with that of Ḥet.

In the Arabic script, a dot was added under the letter called Ji:m ـجـ . This letter joins on both its sides. When it stands alone, its form is larger and the dot appears inside its big curve ج . In certain Arabic dialects such as the Egyptian, the letter is pronounced */g/*, resembling the modern Hebrew Gimel, while in other dialects, such as that of Palestine, it may be pronounced */j/* (as in the English word 'generous'), or as an emphatic sound resembling */q/*.

ج
C
G

د ذ *Da:l, D̲a:l* D

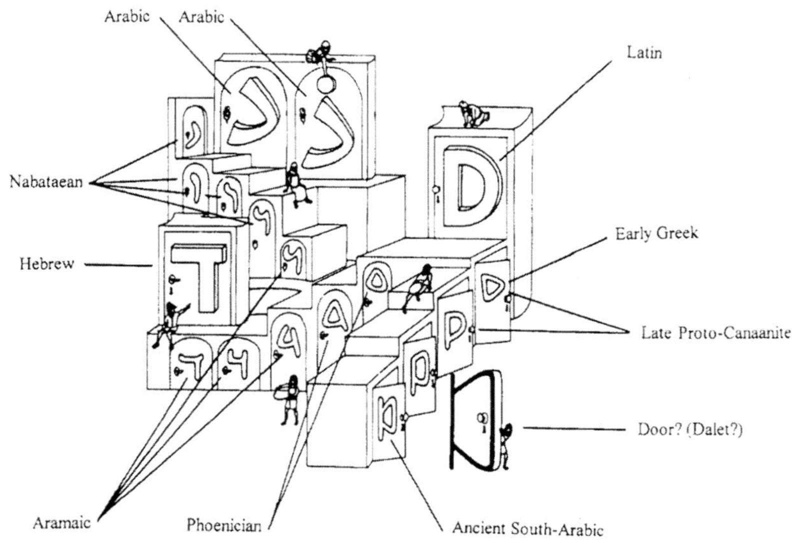

ד *Dalet*

The name of this letter in Hebrew is Dalet, and certain scholars relate this name to the word *Delet*, meaning **door**. A form somewhat resembling a door appears in the South-Arabic script, which seems to have evolved from the early Canaanite script in about the 13th century BCE, before the direction of writing was fixed. No evidence has been discovered so far of the early stages of its evolution, and the earliest South-Arabic inscriptions are not earlier in date than the mid-first millennium BCE. According to certain scholars, the early Dalet had different shapes. In the proto-Canaanite inscriptions from Ṣerabit el-Khadim, dating from the first half of the 2nd millennium BCE, it appears in the form of a **fish** (Hebrew *dag*). In other early Canaanite inscriptions, dating from the 12th or 11th centuries BCE, it has the shape of a triangle ∇ . This sign, which grew a short "tail" in the Phoenician script, retained its triangular shape in the Greek Delta Δ . In early Greek inscriptions, the letter appears in various shapes; in certain examples of the Greek script, one of the angles of the triangle became curved D , and this was

the form of the letter in the Latin script. The letter designating the consonant */d/* is known by different names in the different languages using the Latin script.

In the Aramaic script, which began to show independent features in about the 8th century BCE, the inherited Phoenician triangular Dalet opened up on top, and in the course of time it straightened out and stood upright, and in this form passed into the "Jewish" script.

In the Nabataean cursive script, Dalet lost all its protrusions and became a curved downstroke, open to its left side) . The curve bent in its centre د and the sign continued to exist in this form in the Arabic script where it is called Da:l د . This letter is pronounced */d/*, similarly to the Hebrew Dalet and the English D, but, with a dot above it ذ , it designates a softer sound - */d̲/* - resembling the sound “th” in the word 'the' in English. In Arabic, these two letters join only on the right side and their form does not change in the final position in the word.

ه *Ha:'*

E

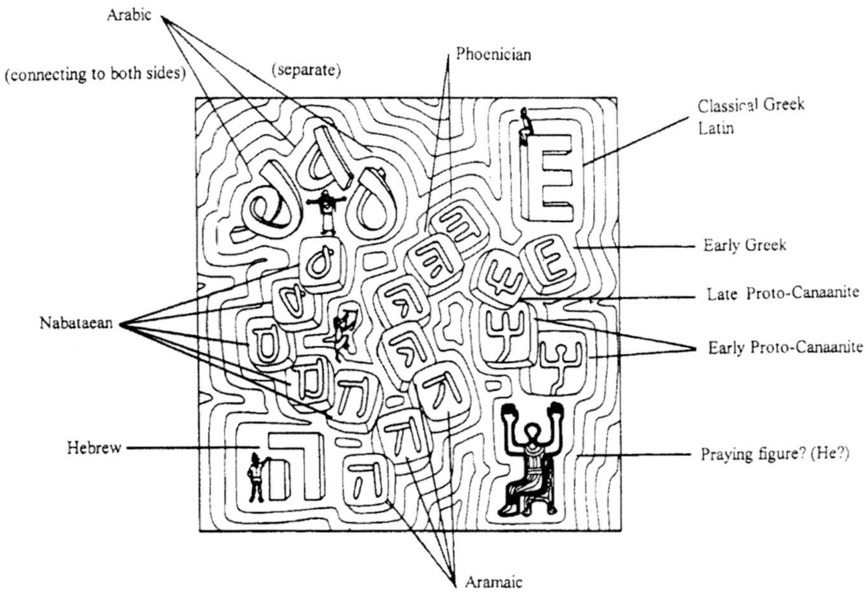

ה *He*

The fifth letter in the Hebrew and Latin alphabets may have evolved from the picture of a **praying figure**. The earliest version of a pictogram of this kind appears in inscriptions dating from about the 19th century BCE, recently discovered in Wadi el-Hol in Egypt, and a later version appears in Proto-Canaanite inscriptions dating from one or two centuries later. The origin of the name of the letter (He in Hebrew) is unknown. It has been suggested that the sound */h/* may perhaps be connected with a certain sound, e.g., 'ho', uttered while praying.

In Arabic the order of letters differs from the Hebrew one, and the letter Ha:' appears in third place from the end. This order of letters is late, however. Canaanite inscriptions dating from the 12th or 11th century BCE display an order of letters resembling that of Hebrew, although not precisely, while an earlier Ugaritic tablet, dating from about the 14th century BCE, bears an abecedarium in almost the same order as in Hebrew. The order of letters in an early Greek abecedarium also resembles that of these earlier finds. Other evidence of a similar order of letters may be found in some Biblical psalms arranged in acrostic order.

The form of He already changed in the Canaanite script , with the omission of some of the strokes and the retaining of only the 'neck' and the raised 'arms'. The Phoenicians were responsible for the fixing of its position . The right-hand downstroke, connecting the other three strokes, extended beyond its join with the lower left stroke.

Having adopted the Canaanite script before the direction of the letter-signs was fixed, the ancient Greeks determined the position of their letters at a later period. Latin received this sign opening to the right E . In the languages using the Latin script, E has different phonetic qualities, and it also serves as a vowel; its name is pronounced differently in each of the languages.

In the Aramaic script, the form of the letter changed in the course of time: the two lower strokes separated from the vertical stroke and combined into one stroke which emerged from the meeting points of the other two strokes , later moving leftwards and hanging down from the upper stroke which gradually became almost horizontal .

In the "Jewish" script, the left downstroke gradually became an independent small stroke, almost parallel to the right-hand stroke ה .

In the Nabataean script, the right downstroke slowly curved at the bottom to the left in the direction of writing > , finally joining the left downstroke. In rapid writing, the writing implement was not always raised between the drawing of the various strokes and the letter gradually came to be written in one continuous stroke, creating a closed loop . This is the form of the Arabic Ha:' when it does not connect to the immediately preceding or following letters. It is the most variable letter-sign in the Arabic script, having five different forms, according to its place in the word: 1. The form of the letter when separate is a circle or a loop with two 'horns' ه ة ; 2. When connecting to the immediately preceding letters, it has an additional stroke on its right-hand side ـه . 3. The form connecting to the left resembles a snail هـ . 4. and 5. When connecting on both sides, the printed form is made up of two circles, one above the other ـهـ , while the form of the letter in handwriting resembles an angle pointing downwards and descending below the line . Its sound in Arabic is */h/* as in Hebrew.

و *Wau*

F

U

V

W

Y

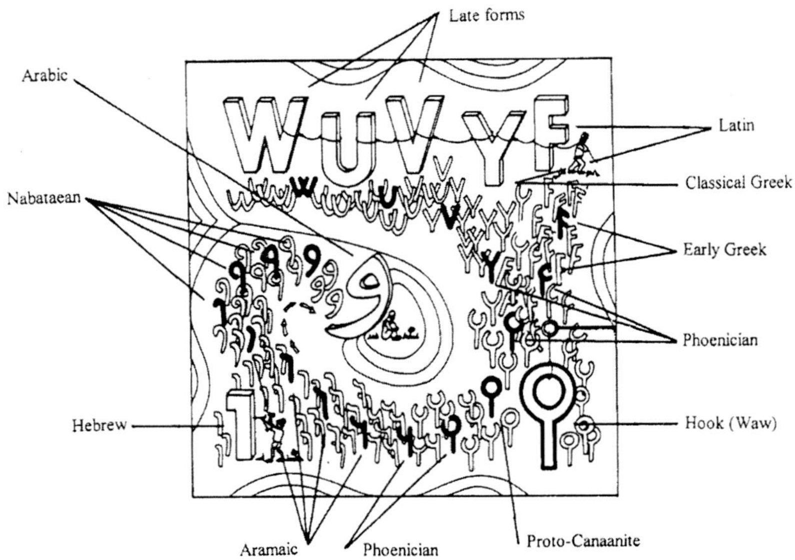

ו *Waw*

As is shown by its Hebrew name, this letter derived from the picture of a **hook** (Hebrew *waw*). This is the pictogram identified as Waw in the Proto-Canaanite inscriptions ϙ dating from the first half of the 2nd millennium BCE as well as in later Canaanite inscriptions.

In Phoenician inscriptions dating from the 11th century BCE, the circle at the top of the sign is open. In the 10th century BCE, two forms of the letter-sign may be discerned: 1. A vertical stroke with two 'arms' at its top spreading upwards and outwards Y ; 2. A vertical stroke with an 'arm' curving to the left on its upper half 𐤅.

In the early Greek script, one finds, amongst others, the form Ϝ , which apparently evolved from the first of the two forms mentioned above. In the Latin alphabet this is the form of the sixth letter. It does not exist in the classical Greek alphabet. On the other hand, the Greeks needed a sign to designate the vowel */u/* and adopted from the Phoenicians the letter Y , which appears in Greek in the

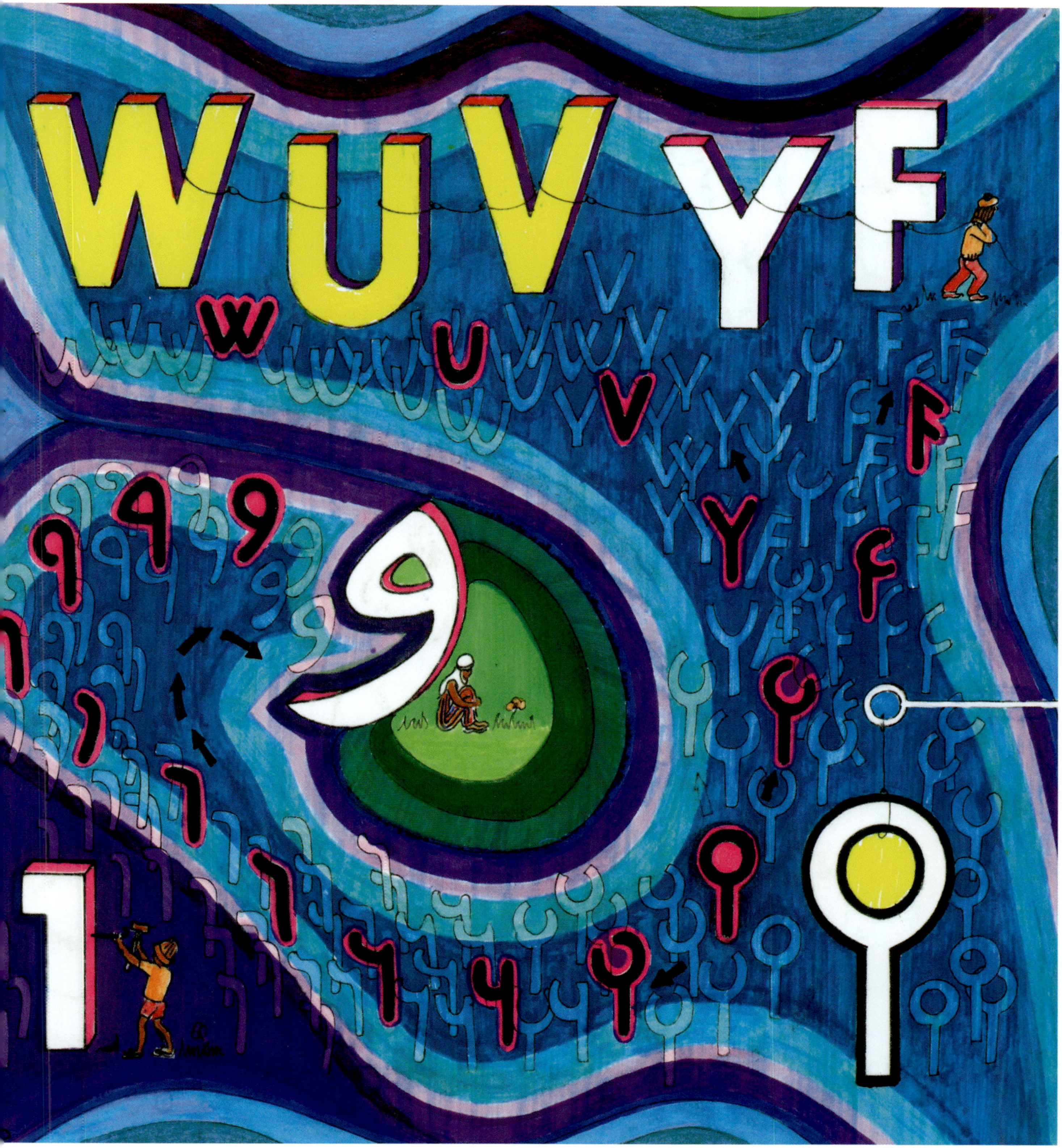
WUV YF

forms Y and V . The Latin script adopted the second of these two signs to designate /u/ and /v/, and in the course of time they also adopted another variant of Waw to designate the letter Y, which took its place among the final letters of the Latin alphabet. Only in the Middle Ages were the letters U and later W added to the Latin alphabet in order to distinguish between the various consonants and vowels. The fact that the Latin language contains more sounds that the Hebrew language is the reason for the larger number of script signs in the Latin alphabet, despite the fact that both use the same writing system. Thus, the Canaanite Waw gave birth to five letters in the Latin writing system: 1. F; 2. Y; 3. V; 4. U; 5. W; their names and pronunciations differ according to the language.

Aramaic adopted and developed the second form of the Phoenician Waw 𐤅 . In the course of time, the left 'arm' straightened out, forming almost a right angle with the vertical stroke 𐡅 . Later this 'arm' was shortened ו , and this became the form of Waw in the "Jewish" script.

A short stroke, emerging at the top of the letter, curved in the Nabataean script 6 𐢋 and became a closed loop 𐢌 . In the Nabataean cursive script, the vertical downstroke curved at the bottom in the direction of writing و , creating the Arabic letter Wau و .

In Arabic and in certain Hebrew dialects which either retain an ancient pronunciation or are influenced by Arabic, this letter is pronounced similarly to the English W, the air freely passing between the teeth and the lips.

ز *Za:i'*

Z

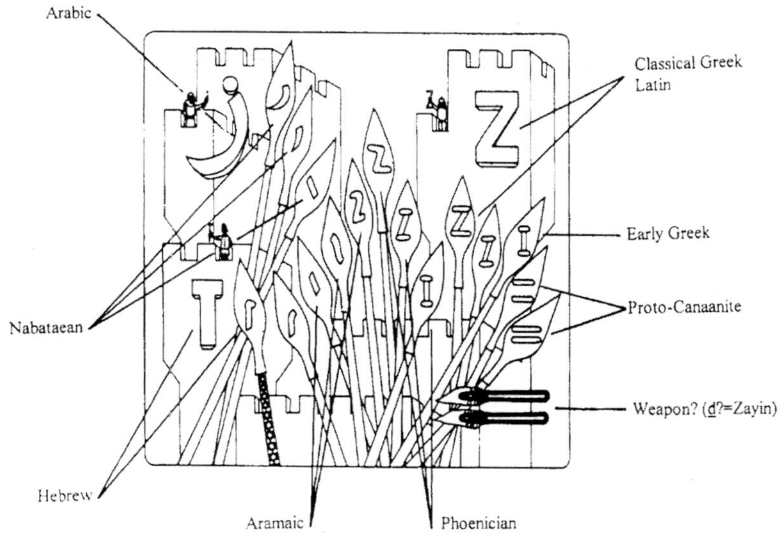

Zayin

The Phoenician alphabet appears to have contained 22 letters, corresponding to 22 different sounds. The early Canaanite language, which used alphabetic signs before the Phoenician, seems to have contained a larger number of sounds than the Phoenician. This conclusion was reached as a result of a comparative study of a group of languages which probably originated in a common ancestor called Proto-Semitic. The estimated original number of sounds is about twenty-nine. This is the number of sounds in Arabic, and it is therefore assumed that the number of sounds used in the much later Arabic language reflects the number of sounds in Proto-Semitic. It is presumed that in Phoenician certain groups of two or three sounds merged together, which is the reason for the smaller number of signs used in writing this language.

Thus, for example, the sounds */z/* and */d̲/* appear as different signs in Canaanite inscriptions dating from before the 11th century BCE: */d̲/* appears as two parallel lines = (the object they describe is unknown), while */z/* appears in the form of an axe , which was perhaps used as a **weapon**, as is indicated by the Hebrew name of the letter Zayin ('weapon'). In the South-Arabic script the sign for Zayin is 𐩸 , while the sign for /ḏ/ is 𐩹 . In Phoenician, both sounds merged, becoming one sound represented by the sign for /ḏ/.

Already in about the 12th century BCE, this letter was written as two parallel short strokes connected by a longer stroke ⊢⊣ . In the early Phoenician script, the letter stands upright I , and so it also appears in the early Greek script. In both these scripts, a process occurred whereby all three strokes were drawn without interruption, creating the form Z . No /z/ sound existed in Latin and the letter G was created instead as the seventh letter in the alphabet. Only when the Romans adopted Greek words containing the sound /z/ was the letter added at the end of the Roman alphabet. The pronunciation of this letter differs in the different languages, and while in English Z is pronounced like the Hebrew Zayin, in German it is pronounced /ts/.

In the Aramaic script, the form of the letter continued to change, its angles gradually curved ז > ז , and in the course of time its form dwindled into a simple downstroke ן . When its form became almost identical to that of Waw, the two letters could be distinguished by the bending of their tops - the top of Waw bending forwards, while the top of Zayin bent backwards ז . This was the form of the letter in the "Jewish" script in about the 2nd century BCE. The hammer-like form T appearing in certain Hebrew script styles emerged at a later period, around the mid-1st millennium CE.

In the Nabataean cursive script, the vertical downstroke gradually curved at the bottom in the direction of writing ر . When adopted for writing in the Arabic language, the form of Zayin resembled that of Resh, and in order to distinguish between the two, a diacritical point was placed above it ز . In Arabic this letter is called Za:i' and it is pronounced in a similar way to the Hebrew Zayin and the English Z. It is not joined to the letter immediately following on its left.

Z
T

ح خ *Ḥa:', Kha:'*

H

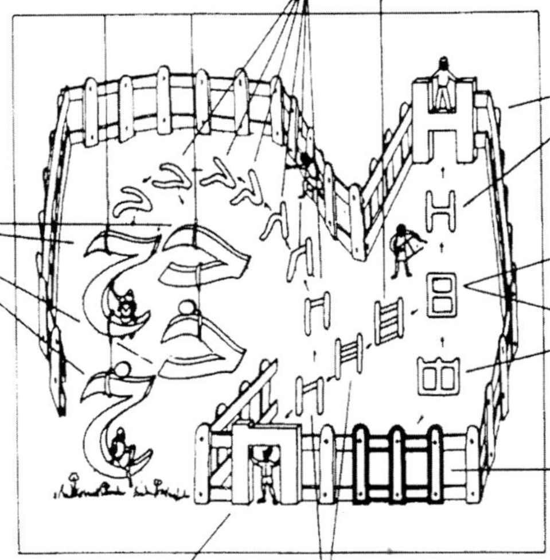

ח *Ḥet*

The form of Ḥet evolved from an early sign, apparently depicting a **fence** ⊏⊐ ⊟. No convincing interpretation has so far been offered for the name Ḥet. The sign stands for two Phoenician sounds, each of which apparently had its own picture in the Proto-Canaanite alphabet. The two sounds, which merged in the Phoenician language, were a guttural sound and a velar sound. In the ancient South-Arabic script, these two sounds are designated by two different signs. According to the accepted theory, the South-Arabic script branched off before the number of signs was reduced in the Canaanite script.

In the Greek script, two outer lines of the halved rectangle fell off, creating the form H of the letter Eta. The Romans later adopted this form for the writing of Latin. In most languages using the Latin script, the pronunciation of this letter resembles that of the Hebrew He rather than that of Ḥet. To express the pronunciation of the guttural Ḥet in the Latin script, a dot is added beneath the letter Ḥ (*/ḥ/*) while the velar sound is indicated by */ḫ/* or */kh/*.

In the Aramaic script, two of the three original parallel lines gradually fell away and only the upper line remained as a bar

between the two vertical "legs" . This form was inherited almost unchanged by the "Jewish" script ח.

In the Nabataean cursive script, Ḥet continued to change its form. In rapid and spontaneous writing, the letter was drawn without lifting the implement from the writing surface. In this way, the upper, horizontal bar joined the left "leg" and together they became one wavy stroke . Since the letter was drawn without interruption from right to left, the right "leg" was drawn downwards and back upwards . This caused the left stroke to gradually slip downwards, along the right "leg" .

In general, the drawing of a stroke directly upwards is much more difficult than drawing it downwards, and it involves a change in the way the writing instrument is held. This difficulty is a major reason for the changes occurring in the form of the letters in rapid writing. In order to shorten the process of drawing the letter, the connecting line was often drawn only half-way upwards , gradually changing its angle with the right-hand stroke > . At the same time, the right-hand downstroke slowly bent forward in the direction of writing, creating the Arabic Ḥa:' حـ . When not connecting to the letter immediately following, a large curve is drawn at the bottom of Ḥa:' ح against the direction of writing.

Already in the Nabataean script, which was mainly used to write Nabataean Aramaic, the form of this letter became identical to that of Gimel, but in the Arabic script they were distinguished by diacritical points, and a dot was added under the letter Ji:m. Since Nabataean Aramaic had only one Ḥet sound, Arabic needed another sign to distinguish between the guttural sound and the velar sound. A dot was therefore placed above the letter in the Arabic script in order to designate the velar Kha:' خـ. All three Arabic letters – Jim, Ḥa:' and Kha:' – can join the letters on either side.

ط ظ *Ṭa:’, Ṯ̣a:’*

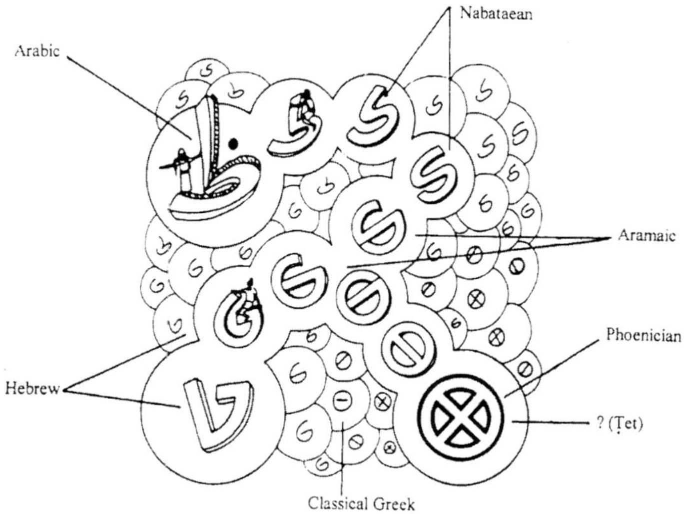

ט *Ṭet*

In Canaanite inscriptions, as well as in early Phoenician inscriptions, the letter Ṭet takes the form of a cross inside a circle ⊗. It resembles the form of a **wheel**, but the origin of the name Ṭet has not yet been discovered.

The Greek letter designating the voiceless */th/* (as in the English word ‘thing’) evolved from the Canaanite sign for Ṭet, as is shown by its Greek name Theta; the cross lost one of its strokes and the other was shortened and became horizontal Θ.

In Latin and in modern languages using the Latin script this letter does not exist.

In early Aramaic inscriptions, Ṭet appears as a circle divided by a slanting line ⊘. In a later phase of its evolution, the circle opened up at the top and the left curve gradually straightened 6 > 6. Already in the 3rd century BCE a form of Ṭet appears in which the slanting line is separated from the left-hand side of the letter ט, creating the form adopted by the “Jewish” script ט.

Hebrew inscriptions pre-dating the 3rd century BCE, and occasionally also later Hebrew inscriptions are written in the ancient Hebrew script, which, like the Aramaic script, derived from the Phoenician script. This ancient Hebrew script, usually called *Da^{c}ats* or *Ra^{c}ats*, is the ancestor of the Samaritan script, which is in use until today. The term “Jewish” script designates the script found in Jewish manuscripts and inscriptions of the Second Temple period. This script, also called “Assyrian” or “square” script, evolved in Judaea as a local script derived from the official Aramaic script of the Persian Empire after its fall to Alexander the Great in the late 4th century BCE.

In the Nabataean script, which evolved from the Aramaic script at about the same time as the “Jewish” script, the slanting line of Ṭet did not separate from the left-hand side of the letter. However, the order of drawing the lines changed when, in rapid writing, the letter was written with a to-and-fro movements  . This form, which changed into  and then  , gave birth to the Arabic Ṭa:’ ط.

This sign, with the addition of a diacritical point above it ظ , also designates another sound in Arabic. This sound possibly existed in the sound system of the Proto-Semitic language as reconstructed by scholars, but its early pronunciation is no longer known. In Arabic it is articulated as an emphatic /ḏ/, with the rear part of the tongue raised. In phonetic transcriptions it may appear as /ṭ/ or /ẓ/. The Arabic Ṭa:’ and Ṯ̣a:’ may join the immediately preceding letters as well as the letters immediately following, and their form is identical in medial and final positions in the word.

ي *Ya:'*

I, J

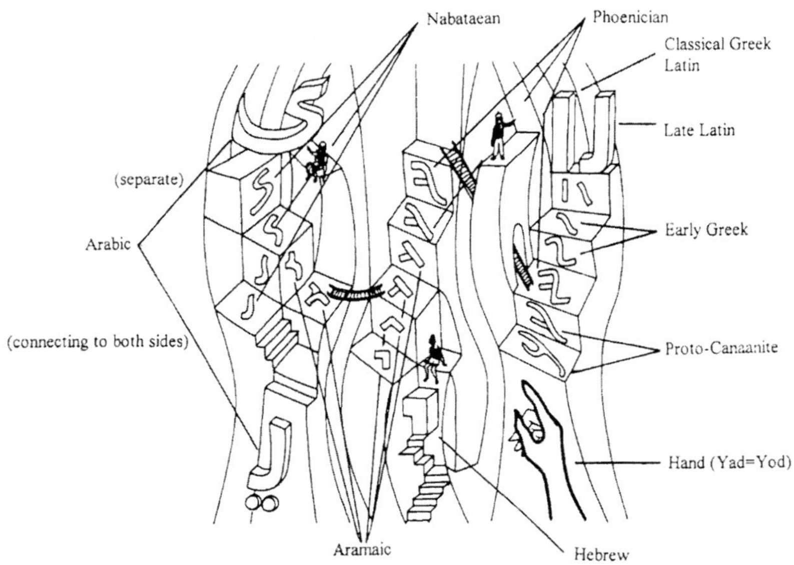

י *Yod*

According to most scholars, the early form of Yod depicted a **hand** with part of the arm seen from the side. A linear sign reminiscent of a hand appears in early Canaanite inscriptions, while a more developed form of it appears in early Phoenician inscriptions dating from about the 11th century BCE.

In the Greek script, this form lost its 'thumb' and what remained was a zigzag which gradually straightened until only a vertical downstroke remained | . This form became part of the Latin script and its name and phonetic expression vary between the different languages using this script. This letter was used to designate a consonant as well as a vowel, as in modern Hebrew, but in the Middle Ages another sign J , a variant of the former, was added to designate the consonant. This sign, too, has various names and expressions in the different languages using the Latin script. The Greek name for I is Yota, resembling the Hebrew name of the letter, Yod.

The Aramaic script retained the 'thumb' for a longer period while the zigzag straightened and grew shorter > > . In the time of the Persian Empire, when Aramaic was the lingua franca, changes occurred in the form of the Aramaic letters despite their use as the official script throughout the empire. The co-existence of several forms of one letter in one and the same style of script could indicate that no strict tradition of Aramaic script styles yet existed. Thus, for example, there was more than one way to draw the Yod: with two strokes or with a single, uninterrupted line . One of these forms gave birth to the angular form > from which the "Jewish" Yod later evolved. This became the smallest letter in the modern Hebrew script י .

The Nabataean script favoured the form drawn with one continuous movement. In the course of time, various forms of the letter emerged in the Nabataean cursive script; one of these was the ancestor of the final form of Ya:' in Arabic ى, while a smaller variant, which may join the letters on the right and left , is used in a medial position. In a certain phase of its evolution, this variant became identical in form with the cursive Ba:', Nu:n and Ta:', and in order to distinguish it from the identical forms, two diacritical points, or sometimes a short horizontal line were added beneath the Ya:' ﻴ ﻴ .

ك *Ka:f*

K

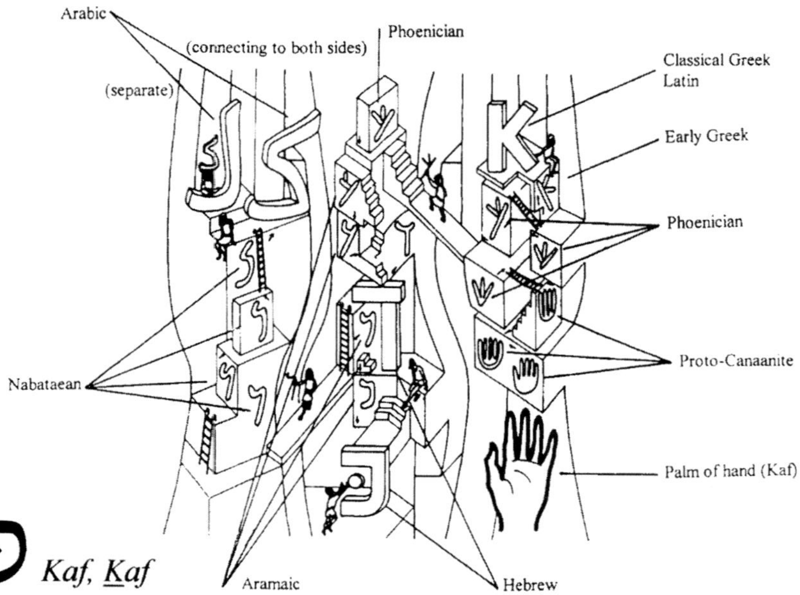

כּ,כ,ך *Kaf, K̲af*

One of three pictograms appearing in an ancient inscription discovered at the site of the Biblical Gezer, as well as the name of the letter – Kaf – meaning '**palm of the hand**', bear witness to the ancient form of the letter: an open hand with five fingers. Already in the inscriptions found at Ṣerabit el-Khadim in the Sinai peninsula, dating from the first half of the second millennium BCE, linear forms of Kaf appear with four and with three fingers . In Canaanite inscriptions dating from about the 12th century BCE, two forms of Kaf are found: one with three fingers and a long "leg" , and another with three fingers without the "leg" .

In the ancient Greek script, the two forms mentioned above were used at a certain period to designate two different sounds. The form without the "leg" went out of use while the "fingers" in the other form changed direction . The "leg" gradually shortened and became a vertical downstroke. The Latin script retains this form, which opens to the right K and its use as a non-vocal, velar stop is quite similar in most languages employing the Latin script.

The Aramaic script inherited the form with the "leg" from the Phoenician script. In about the late 5th century BCE, in the beginning and middle of a word, the 'long-legged' letters (Kaf, Mem, Nun, Pe and Ṣadi), when written rapidly with a brush and ink, began to curve at the bottom leftwards in the direction of writing. Thus, the final forms of these letters (except for the final Mem) are actually the earlier forms, while the initial and medial forms represent a later phase of their evolution.

Already in the Aramaic script of the 5th century BCE, the middle "finger" of Kaf moved toward the tip of the left, lower "finger" 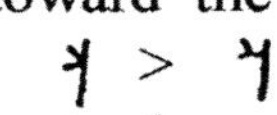 . It was a short step from here to the creation of the final and medial forms of Kaf in the "Jewish" script in about the 3rd century BC 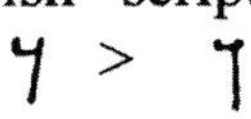 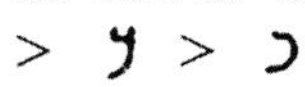
A group of six letters – Bet, Gimel, Dalet, Kaf, Pe and Taw – have a unique characteristic in Hebrew and Aramaic: these letters represent different sounds according to their place in the word. A diacritic dot appearing inside the letter in Hebrew indicates a plosive articulation as against a fricative articulation when it is written without the dot. The phonetical transcription of the fricative Kaf is /k̲/. In Hebrew the dot is called Dagesh.

Unlike the "Jewish" script, which eventually retained the final forms of only five letters (Kaf, Mem, Nun, Pe, and Ṣadi), the Nabataean script used final forms of most of the letters: i.e., Alef, Bet, He, Waw, Yod, Kaf, Lamed, Mem, Nun, Ayin, Pe, Ṣadi and Qof. These forms were used inconsistently and some of them disappeared but this feature also characterizes the Arabic script. Some of the Arabic final forms emerged within the Arabic script and were not inherited from the Nabataean forms. Thus, for example, the final Ka:f in the Arabic script  evolved independently toward the late first millennium, while the medial form of the Arabic Ka:f 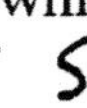 evolved from the cursive Nabataean script; the upper part of the letter gradually grew longer 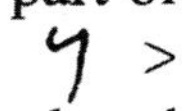 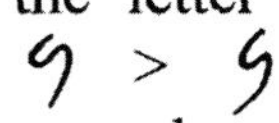 while the "leg" shortened and curved to the left in the direction of writing at the bottom 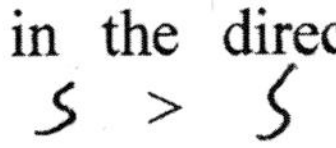 .
Unlike Hebrew, which distinguishes between a plosive and a fricative Kaf, there is only one sound of Kaf in Arabic, which is pronounced like K in English.

K

ل *La:m* L

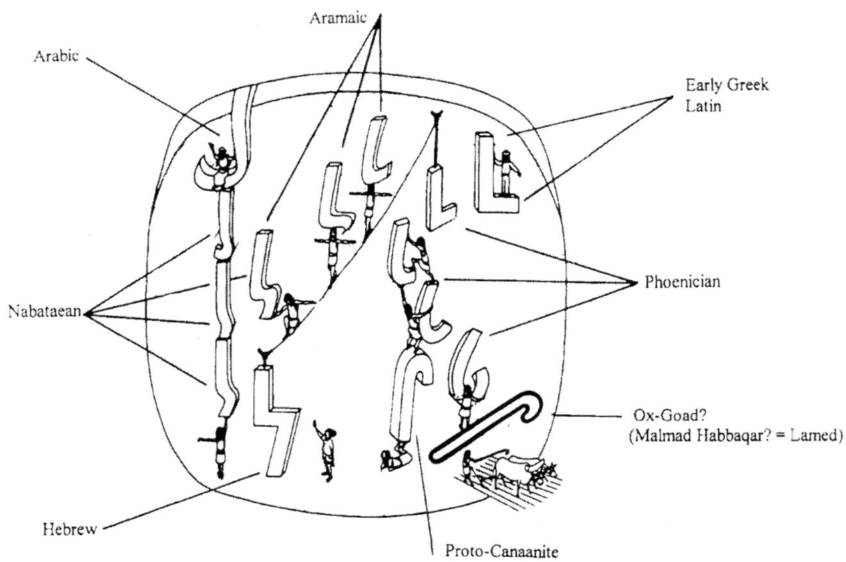

ל *Lamed*

The Bible (Judges 3:31) mentions the words *malmad-habbaqar* (**ox-goad**), the word *malmed* deriving from the root *lmd* (Hebrew, 'to learn', 'to teach'). It has been suggested that this was the origin of the pictogram of Lamed , appearing in Canaanite inscriptions in the form of a bent stick. The position and direction of the pictogram vary from one Canaanite inscription to the other. In about the 13th or the 12th century BCE, the form of the letter resembled a snail rather than a stick, but already in the 11th century the snail-form opened up again . In the Phoenician script it already appears in the form of a line slanting down in a leftwards direction and bending back at the bottom to the right . Already in early Phoenician inscriptions, the letter is higher than other letters.

In the early Greek script, this letter appears in various positions , while in the classical Greek script Lambda resembles an isosceles triangle without the base Λ. The Romans adopted the form of a right-angle facing to the right L, and this is the form of L in the Latin script.

In the Aramaic script, the form of Lamed remained almost unchanged until approximately the 4th century BCE, when a small 'tail' emerged at its lower right extremity as a result of drawing the writing instrument to the left towards the letter immediately following  . From this form evolved the "Jewish" Lamed, already to be found in the early Dead Sea Scrolls dating from the late 3rd and early 2nd centuries BCE .

A similar form appears in Nabataean inscriptions and manuscripts, mostly in the final position  . One also finds a more developed form in which the original angle became a wavy line while the additional 'tail' gradually became an almost horizontal base-stroke  drawn towards the letter immediately following.

This form gave birth to the Arabic La:m  . In Arabic this letter may connect to both the immediately preceding and following letters. It extends above the line like the Hebrew Lamed.

م *Mi:m*

M

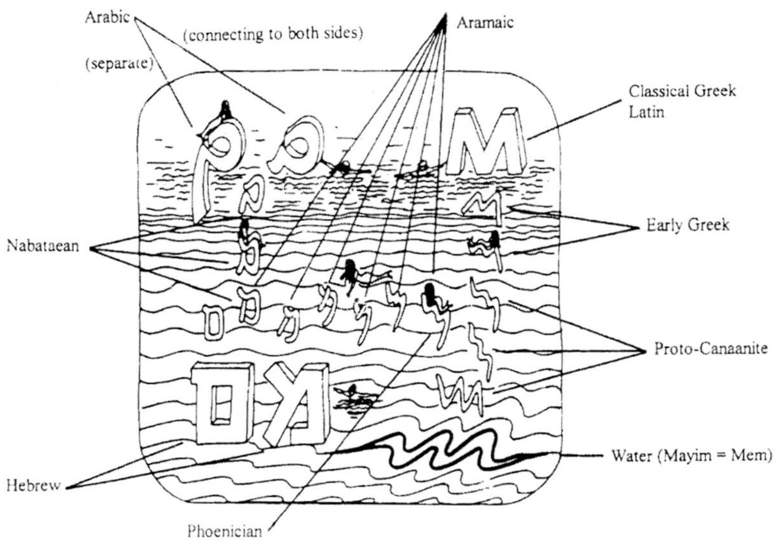

מ,ם *Mem*

As indicated by its Hebrew name and its zigzagging form , the original pictogram of Mem apparently represented **water**. Already in Canaanite inscriptions dating from approximately the 13th or 12th century BCE and in early Phoenician inscriptions, one finds the zigzag in an upright position . The Greek script appears to have adopted the horizontal form. In the course of time, the zigzag shortened and became more angular , until only four strokes remained M . The Romans adopted this form and it became part of the Latin alphabet, indicating the nasal sound */m/*.

The Aramaeans inherited the Phoenician Mem in the phase when it had a long "tail" slanting down on its right side in the direction of writing . The Aramaic Mem underwent a change and came to be drawn with two movements rather than one uninterrupted zigzag. This was the form of the Aramaic Mem in about the late 6th century BCE, and already in the 5th century the additional left-hand downstroke lengthened while the right-hand downstroke started to curve to the left in the direction of writing  >  .

In the course of time, the original left serif became a separate short stroke on the upper left-hand side of the letter  >  .

In the "Jewish" script, one finds a final Mem, which was created when the curved right-hand downstroke was drawn toward the left vertical downstroke  >  >  .

The Nabataean final Mem  was created in a similar way. The curved right-hand stroke continued upwards until it touched the "roof" at the point where the left-hand downstroke emerges. In the course of time, the letter became smaller in relation to the other letters  , and it was drawn like a circle with an additional stroke slanting down to the left towards the letter immediately following  . At this stage of its evolution, the remains of the early serif disappeared. This is the form of the Arabic Mi:m when it joins to the left. It may join the preceding or the following letters in various ways , and sometimes only a dot or a bend remains to testify to its existence. The Arabic final Mi:m evolved independently from the medial form  . The left-hand downstroke lengthened and the letter somewhat resembles the final Mem in the Hebrew modern cursive script, a form apparently created in the late Middle Ages.

ن *Nu:n* N

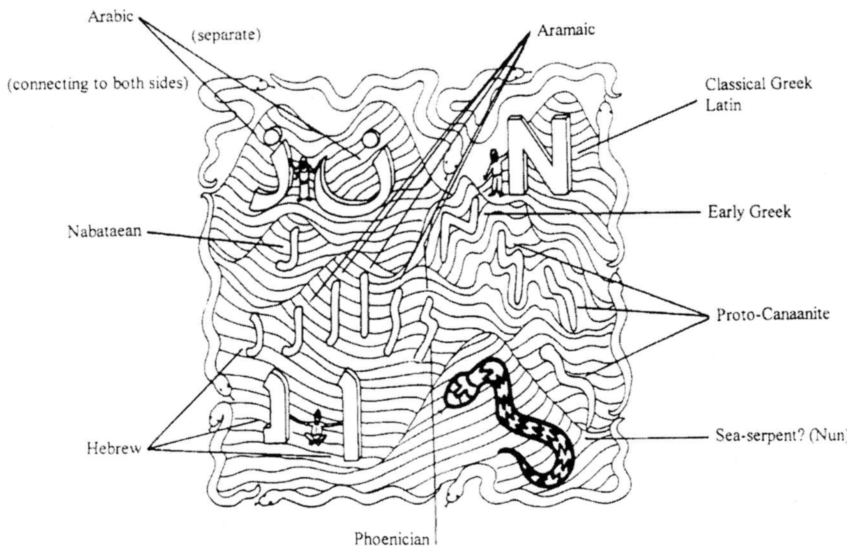

נ,ן *Nun*

In ancient Canaanite inscriptions, scholars have identified a pictogram resembling a snake as the early form of Nun, although the word Nun in Aramaic means 'fish' (perhaps a **sea serpent**? The word for snake in Hebrew - *naḥash* - also begins with Nun). In Phoenician inscriptions of the 10th century BCE onwards only minor changes occurred in the form of the letter which may be described as a zigzag of three strokes in an upright position 𐤍 , the length of the strokes varying in the course of time.

The Greek script adopted the letter before the direction of writing was fixed. When the Latin script adopted the sign, its upper and lower strokes had already become two vertical parallel strokes connected by a diagonal running down from left to right N . This form of the capital N has been retained in the Latin script through the ages.

In the Aramaic script, Nun had a long "leg"  , and, in the same way as with the other "long-legged" letters (except for Mem), a medial form of the letter was created in about the late 5th or early 4th century BCE, when the "leg" curved leftwards at the bottom in the direction of writing and the top bent backwards  . The "Jewish" script inherited both the medial and final forms of Nun. The bending to the left of the top of the Hebrew Nun is a later phenomenon.

In the extreme cursive Nabataean script style, the medial Nun became identical in its form to Bet, Yod and Taw. Only in about the 8th century CE, when the Arabic script was used for the writing of the Islamic sacred scriptures, were diacritical points added in order to distinguish between these letters. That is the reason why the reading of early Arabic inscriptions and manuscripts not containing diacritical points is extremely difficult.

The Arabic Nu:n has one dot above it. When written separately, it takes the form of a concave curve with a dot above it ن .

X

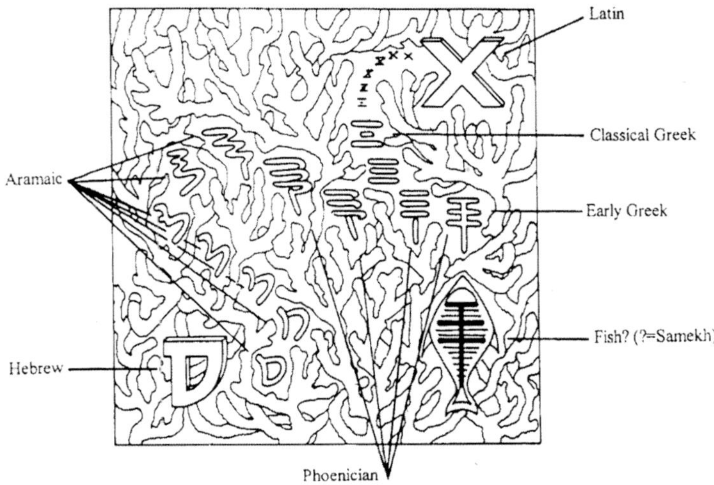

ס *Samekh*

The early form of Samekh is unknown. In Arabic, the word *samak* means 'fish' (Hebrew *shemek̲*); the sign of Samekh in the South-Arabic script is somewhat reminiscent of the form of a **fish**, and it may perhaps indicate an earlier form. In a Canaanite inscription from 'Izbet Ṣartah, dating from about the 12th century BCE, in which the letters of the alphabet appear in an order almost similar to that of the Hebrew alphabet, the letter Samekh was identified with a sign resembling a rectangle containing several horizontal lines intersected by a vertical line. A somewhat similar form appears in ancient Greek inscriptions.

The earliest certain evidence of Samekh appears in the Phoenician script of about 1000 BCE. At that period, Samekh appears in the form of three horizontal lines, one above the other, intersected by a long vertical line. In inscriptions from the 8th or 7th century BCE this line occasionally appears as a "leg" emerging from the lowest of the three lines.

In Greek, the sign designated the letter XEI. The vertical line disappeared and the second horizontal line grew shorter Ξ. In early western manuscripts in the Greek script, the letter sometimes appears as two crossing lines X, and this is the form of the Latin X. There is no evidence of the intermediate phases in the evolution of this form, and the reconstruction of these phases is hypothetical. The Romans began to use the sign in about the late 1st century AD, and it therefore appears close to the end of the Latin alphabet. This letter has a variety of phonetical expressions in the different languages using the Latin script.

In the Aramaic script, short "tails" gradually evolved at the right-hand extremities of the three horizontal lines , curving to the left in the direction of writing. Eventually all three lines joined together and formed one winding line ending in a long vertical stroke . In the course of time, the number of upper strokes was reduced while the vertical stroke began to curve leftwards at the bottom  >  > . This was the form of the Aramaic Samekh in about the 5th century BCE. Already at this period, variant forms of the sign appear without the typical zigzag . The top of the letter shortened and slipped downwards, almost touching the end of the curved downstroke on the right , and the letter became smaller and rounder. This was the form adopted by the "Jewish" script as found in Qumran manuscripts of about the 2nd century BCE. The letter gradually closed at the bottom 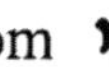 > , producing a form of Samekh which has remained almost unchanged in the Hebrew square script until today.

In the Nabataean script used for the writing of Nabataean Aramaic, a similar form of Samekh appears, but in Arabic it does not exist at all because its sound merged with that of the Arabic Sin.

ع غ *ᶜE:n, Ġe:n* O

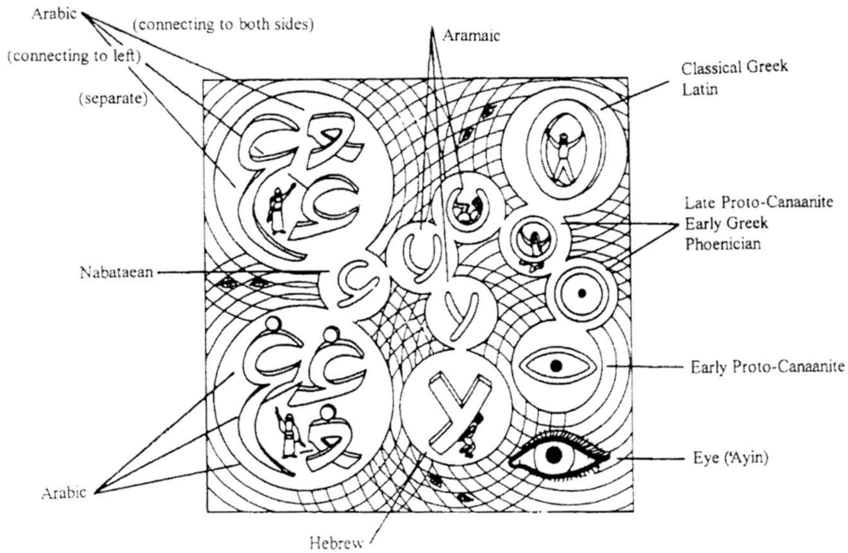

ע *ᶜAyin*

Already in the earliest inscriptions in alphabetic script, dating from about the 19th century BCE, we find the form of an **eye** with its pupil . These inscriptions have recently been discovered in Wadi el-Hol in Egypt and indicate that the so-called Canaanite alphabet actually originated in Egypt. In early Canaanite inscriptions, the 'eye' appears with or without its pupil , while in the ancient Greek script the letter appears as a circle with a dot in the centre ⊙ . In the classical Greek script, the sign appears as a circle without a dot and this is also its form in the Latin script O .

The guttural consonant /ᶜ/ does not exist in the Indo-European languages. It existed in Biblical Hebrew and it exists in Arabic and in the Hebrew spoken by Jews born in Arabic countries. The letter is called ᶜAyin, the Semitic word for 'eye'.

In Phoenician inscriptions, the letter appears as a circle, and this was the form inherited by the Aramaeans. However, the Phoenician ᶜAyin, as well as certain other letters in the Phoenician script, such as Bet, Dalet, and Resh, the upper part of which was formed as a circle or a triangle, opened up at the top in the Aramaic

offshoot of this script  . In the course of time, the curve divided into two strokes, both drawn downwards toward each other  . In this way, a "tail" was created at the bottom of the right-hand stroke, which was drawn to the left in the direction of writing. This stroke gradually became longer.

In the "Jewish" script, ᶜAyin was drawn with two strokes, the left one usually shorter than the right one  , and this was its form already in the Dead Sea scrolls in about the late 3rd and early 2nd century BCE.

The Nabataean ᶜAyin underwent a similar process, but the letter remained closer to the earlier curved form while changing its position until the right stroke became almost horizontal 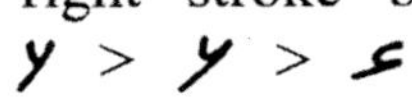 . This was the way the Arabic form of the letter was created عـ . The Arabic ᶜE:n can join the immediately preceding and immediately following letters. When connecting to both sides, it has the form of a tiny triangle standing on its head ـعـ . In a final position, the right-hand base stroke curves back to the right ع against the direction of writing.

In Arabic, another sound is written with the same sign. This sound, resembling a guttural */r/*, apparently existed in Proto-Semitic. A letter representing the same consonant is found in Ugaritic inscriptions dating from about the 14th-12th centuries BCE, as well as in much later South Arabic inscriptions, probably dating from the last centuries BCE and the first centuries CE. Its phonetic transcription may be either */ġ/* or */gh/*, as for example in the name of the city Baghdad. In Hebrew and Aramaic, this sound merged with ᶜAyin, as in the name of the city Gaza, in Hebrew ᶜAzzah. The Arabic letter denoting this sound is called Ġe:n and it is distinguished from ᶜE:n by a diacritical point above it غـ غ .

ف *Fa:'* P

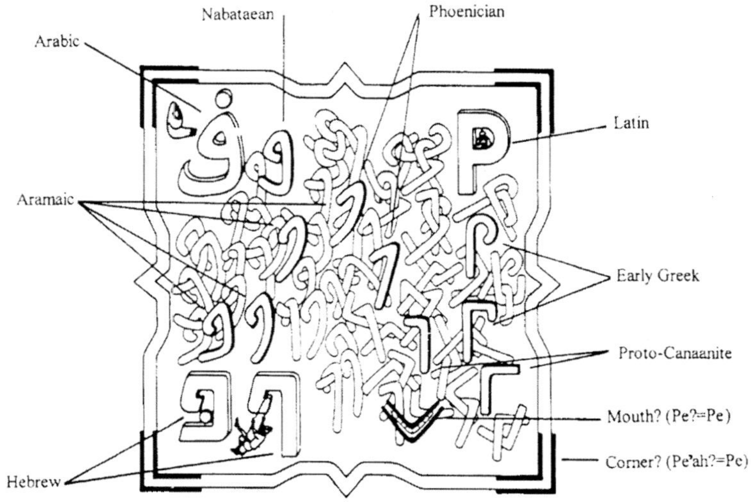

פּ, פ, ף *Pe, Fe*

The pictogram of Pe in the Serabit el-Khadim inscriptions, dating from the first half of the first millennium BCE, has the form of two parallel sections of an arc , or of an angle . A quite similar form appears in the earlier Wadi el-Hol inscriptions, but it is unclear if in these inscriptions it is to be interpreted as Pe or as Gimel. The meaning of the name is unclear. It could perhaps indicate that the original pictogram described a **mouth** (Hebrew *peh*), or perhaps a **corner** (of a field? Biblical Hebrew *pe'ah*). In Canaanite inscriptions of about the 13th or 12th century BCE, the letter appears as one of the upper angles of a high rectangle , and it resembles the sign of Gimel in one of its phases. But already in the early Phoenician inscriptions these two letters tilt at quite a different angle and Pe tends to extend beyond the imaginary base-line. In most of the inscriptions, its top is somewhat curved .

In the early Greek script, the letter stands erect and tends to bend its top . In the course of time, the curved top of the letter became a semicircle , and the position and direction of the letter were fixed P. This is also its form in the Latin script. Its phonetic expression in the languages using the Latin script is quite similar in all cases. In the classical Greek script, however, this form is used for another sound while the sound */p/* is designated by a sign resembling a high rectangle without a base line Π.

The Aramaic medial Pe, like the other "long-legged" letters, began to curve to the left at the bottom in the direction of writing > at about the time when the "Jewish" and Nabataean scripts branched off from the Aramaic cursive script. This is its form in the "Jewish" script; the typical "nose" of the Hebrew letter is a somewhat later development. In the final position in a word, the long form of Pe was retained.

In Hebrew as well as Aramaic, Pe has two phonetic manifestations resembling */p/* and */f/* in English, depending on their place in the word. This dual manifestation formerly existed in these languages in the case of the six letters Bet, Gimel, Dalet, Kaf, Pe and Taw, grammatically known as 'Beged Kefet'. When vowelization marks were added to Hebrew texts in about the 8th century CE, a dot was added within these letters to designate the plosive sounds and to distinguish them from the fricatives. Thus, a dot inside Pe designates the plosive sound */p/*. In modern Sephardic Hebrew, only three out of the six letters (Bet, Kaf, and Pe) have retained the dual phonetic manifestation בּ/ב כּ/כ פּ/פ.

In the Nabataean script, the top of the letter continued to curve while the long "leg" bent to the left in the direction of writing. This form also appears in the final position in a word. Already in the Nabataean script, Pe and Qof became similar in their forms, and in the Arabic script they are identical. In order to distinguish between them, one dot was added above Fa:' ف, while two dots were added above Qa:f ق. In Arabic, only the fricative pronunciation of Pe has been retained and it may be transcribed into English with an f. The sound */p/* does not exist in classical Arabic. Fa:' joins on both its sides to the immediately neighbouring letters, and when it joins to the left, its base-stroke is short ﻓ.

ف
P
פּ
ף

ض ص *Ṣa:d, Ḍa:d*

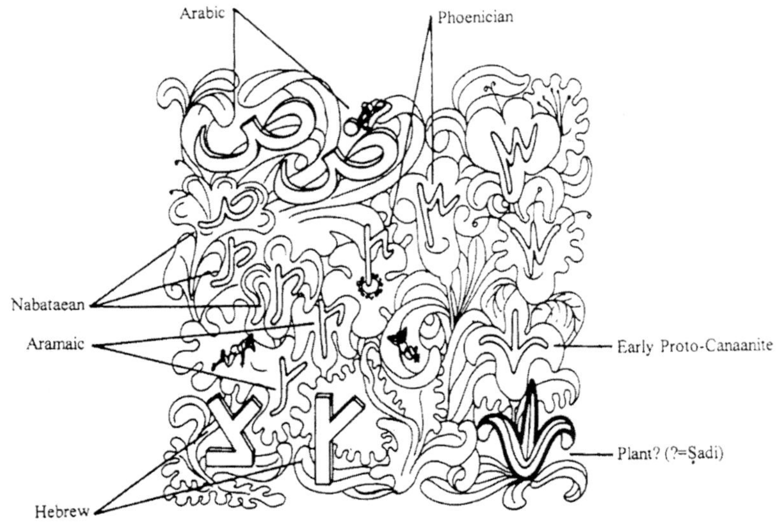

צ, ץ *Ṣadi*

In early Canaanite inscriptions, Ṣadi appears in the form of a **plant** (Hebrew *tsemakh*) or a blossom (Hebrew *tsits*) . A sign in the form of two arms spread out sideways, emerging from a long, vertical "leg" , is found in a Canaanite abecedarium in the inscription from ʻIsbet Ṣartah dating from about the 12th century BCE. This sign has been identified as Ṣadi. The letter appears in inscriptions of about the 11th century BCE in the form of two straight lines, one of which emerges from the centre of the other , or as a more complex sign . It is unclear if these represent two phases in the evolution of one and the same sign, or two different signs. As another sound, which later merged with Ṣadi, apparently existed in the Proto-Canaanite language, some scholars claim that the signs evolved from two different pictograms.

After the reduction in the number of consonants in the Phoenician language, one sign remained which may have been the descendant of the Proto-Canaanite sign. However, the meaning of the name Ṣadi is unknown, and cannot indicate the original picture from which this letter derived.

The sign for Ṣadi, which existed in the early Greek script, later disappeared from the classical Greek alphabet and does not exist in the Latin script.

In Phoenician inscriptions of the 10th century BCE, Ṣadi was written as a short vertical line with a zigzag emerging from its center on the right-hand side 𐤑. By the 9th century BCE, the short stroke had already become longer 𐤑. From this form, various forms of Ṣadi evolved, as seen, for example, in Aramaic documents from Elephantine dating from the 5th century BCE. In all these forms, the former zigzag appears as one or two short strokes on the right side of the vertical long "leg" 𐡑 𐡑 𐡑.

When the various local scripts branched off from the Aramaic, the variant with the T-shaped "arm" 𐡱 was adopted by the Palmyrene script, while the variant with the arm running upwards ץ was adopted by the "Jewish" script, and the variant with the angular arm turning downwards 𐢕 by the Nabataean script.
Like the other "long-legged" letters, the Aramaic Ṣadi also developed a medial form with the leg curving leftwards at the bottom. The "Jewish" script retained the medial and the final צ ץ forms of this letter.
In the Nabataean script, the angular arm became curved, and an oval loop was created on the right side of the vertical stroke 𐢕. At the same time, the vertical stroke curved at the bottom in the direction of writing 𐢖. This form gave birth to the Arabic Ṣa:d ص, pronounced like an emphatic /s/, deep in the throat. Ṣadi belongs to the small group of emphatic consonants whose pronunciation is characteristic of the Semitic languages. Another consonant in this group, which merged with Ṣadi in Hebrew, and with Qof and 'Ayin in Aramaic, survived in Arabic and was designated by the same sign but with a dot above it ض. This sound apparently has no parallel in any modern language; its pronunciation resembles that of /d/ articulated deep in the throat, and, in fact, it is difficult to distinguish its unique pronunciation in the Arabic languages spoken today. (In the Ethiopic alphabet, which apparently evolved from the South-Arabic script, a sign for this consonant exists, but its pronunciation is different from that in Arabic and pertains to the ejective sounds typical of some African languages). The phonetic transcription of Arabic Ṣa:d ص is /ṣ/ and that of Ḍa:d ض is /ḍ/. Both letters join the immediately preceding and the immediately following letters. When joining the letter immediately following, the large curve on the left becomes a short stroke ضـ صـ.

ق *Qa:f*

Q

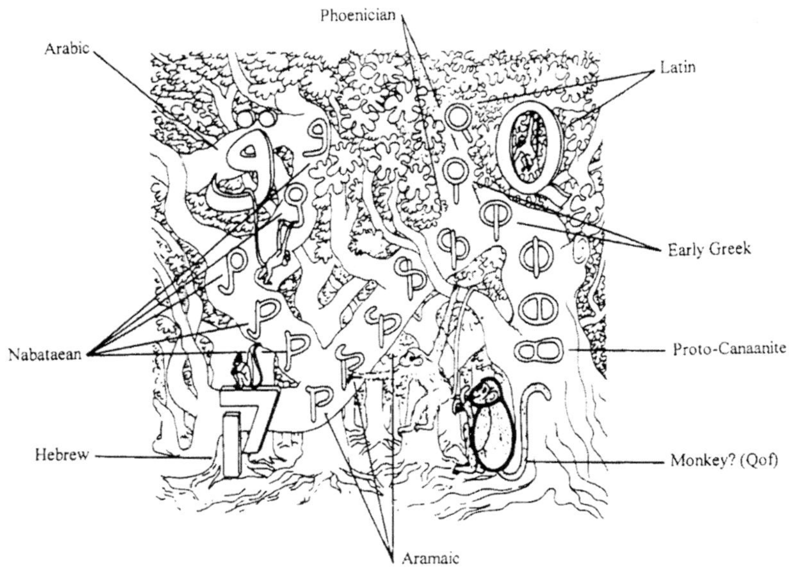

ק *Qof*

The original pronunciation of the names of the letters of the alphabet is unknown. Our pronunciation seems to be a mixed one combining Aramaic and Hebrew and perhaps another west Semitic dialect. The names of some letters in Greek seem to retain an earlier pronunciation, but this does not help in reconstructing the original meaning of the names when this meaning has been lost.

The name of this letter may be interpreted as the name of an animal – **a monkey**, *qof* in Hebrew - or perhaps as the **eye of a needle**, in Hebrew called *quf*. The pictogram identified with Qof in the Proto-Canaanite inscriptions from Sinai consists of two circles of different diameters, one above the other 8. In the Canaanite abecedarium of the ʻIzbet Ṣartah ostracon, dating from about the 12th century BCE, the form of the letter resembles a needle ϙ with a large hole at its top. In the early Greek script, side by side with this form, a variant form appears, in which the vertical stroke cuts through the circle ϙ. This is also the form of the letter in early Phoenician inscriptions.

In the early classical Greek script, this letter did not survive, but it entered the Roman alphabet. In the course of time, the long "leg" shortened and only a short "tail" remained, slanting down to the right at the bottom of a large circle The emphatic quality of the consonant designated by this letter in the Semitic languages does not characterize the corresponding consonant in languages using the Latin script.

In the west-Semitic scripts, the circle at the top of the letter opened up and was drawn with two separate curves opening towards each other . In the course of time, the lower end of the left curve joined the upper end of the right curve , gradually becoming a wavy line on top of the vertical downstroke . The left curve later became shorter while the right curve became somewhat angular , and this form already appears in the Aramaic script of the late 6th century BCE, and later in the "Jewish" script.

At a certain stage of its evolution in the Nabataean script, the form of Qof resembled that of Sadi – a vertical line curving at the bottom to the left, with an oval loop at the top on its right side .

In the cursive script, this letter was written without interruption in one continuous movement, and the small circle at the top gradually moved leftwards > > . In this phase, its form resembled that of Pe, and this was its form in the Arabic alphabet. Since the two letters were indistinguishable, two diacritical points were added on top of Qa:f ق while only one point was added on top of Fa:' ف. Qa:f joins its immediately preceding and following letters, and when it joins the following letter its "leg" is shortened.

This sound is made by touching the uvula with the root of the tongue. Its pronunciation differs from that of ka:f, unlike in modern Hebrew, in which the pronunciation of the two consonants is identical.

ق
Q
ק

ر *Ra:'*

R

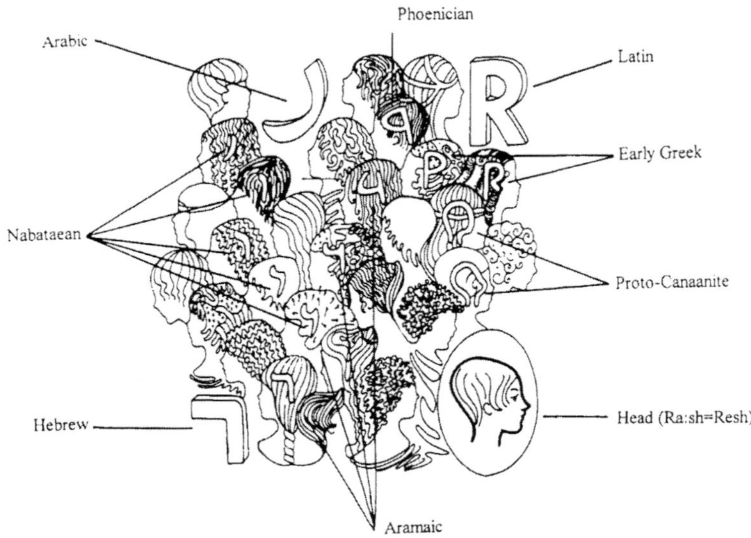

ר *Resh*

Resh is one of the few letters whose origin is incontestable. The picture of a **head** (Hebrew *rosh*) appearing already in the inscriptions from Wadi el-Hol and in those from Ṣerabit el-Khadim , as well as the name Resh, indicating the Aramaic pronunciation of the word, clearly attest to the pictographic identity of this letter. In Canaanite inscriptions dating from about the 12th century BCE, Resh appears as a semicircle, representing the former head, with a straight downstroke on its left side, extending below its base, representing the neck P. This form was retained in the classical Greek script as well as in several other scripts adopting the Greek rather than the Latin forms of the letters, such as the Russian script. In the ancient Greek script, another variant of this letter appears, with a short "tail" emerging from the lower meeting point between the curve and the downstroke R. This is the origin of the Latin R form.

The phonetic expression of the consonant designated by this sign varies among the different languages using the Latin script.

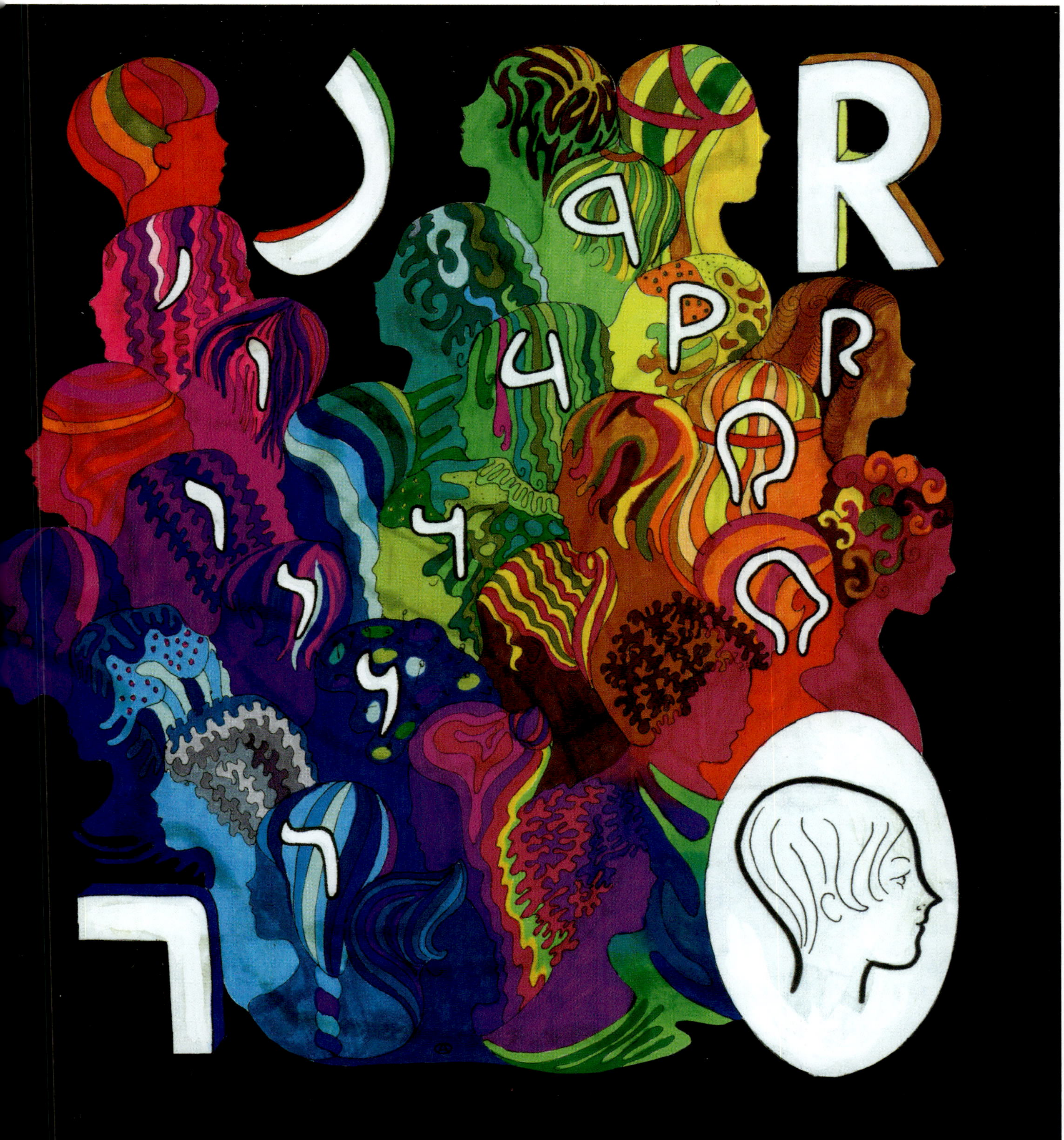

In the early Phoenician script, the "face" turned leftwards and bent forward somewhat 𐤓 . In the Aramaic script its position straightened and its curved top opened up 𐡓 as in the cases of Bet, Dalet and 'Ayin. In the course of time, the concave curve straightened and became an almost horizontal stroke with a short serif on its left extremity 𐡓 > 𐡓 > ר . When it was written as a single interrupted stroke, the "hump" on its right-hand upper corner disappeared ר . This form remained almost unchanged in the "Jewish" script and still exists in the Hebrew 'square' alphabet.

In the cursive Nabataean script, the angular form of Resh became a short curved stroke, very similar in form to Zayin 𐢆 > ر . In the Arabic script, a dot was added on top of Za:i' to distinguish it from Ra:'. Like Za:i', Ra:' does not join the letter immediately following, and its form ر does not change in accordance with its position in the word.

س ش *Shi:n, Si:n* S

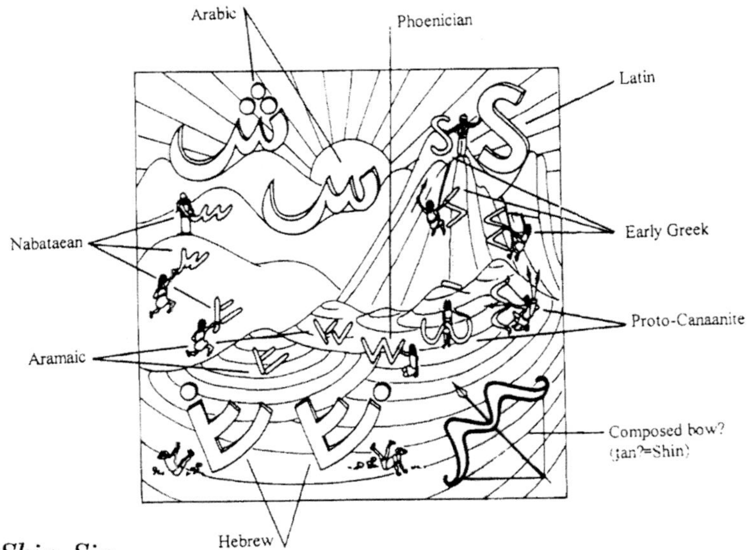

שׁ, שׂ *Shin, Sin*

The picture of a **composed bow** called *than* ᔕ designated the interdental consonant /ṯ/ or /th/ (as, for example, in the English 'thing') in the Proto-Canaanite script, while a triangle with two "horns" (perhaps describing the **rising sun** [Hebrew *shemesh*]?) ⴳ designated the consonant /š/ or /sh/. In the Phoenician language, /th/ merged with /sh/, and this consonant, apparently pronounced /sh/, was designated by the sign depicting the composed bow.

In Canaanite inscriptions dating from about the 12th century BCE, this sign appears in various positions. The erect form ʒ ʒ was adopted by the Greek script. In the classical Greek alphabet, the letter Sigma (*than* > *san*) appears in the form of two adjacent acute angles Σ facing to the right. However, already in the ancient Greek script, more developed forms of this sign ≶ S also appear. The curved form became the letter S of the Latin alphabet. Its phonetic expression, which sometimes depends on the sounds next to it, can vary in the different languages using the Latin script.

In early Phoenician inscriptions, the sign appears standing on both its pointed ends , facing upwards. This is also its form in early Aramaic inscriptions. An intermediate form consisting of only three strokes appears in Aramaic documents written in ink dating from the late 6th century BCE, while in the 5th century BCE, the two right-hand strokes join the left-hand, slanting stroke .

A similar form exists in the "Jewish" script from the 3rd century BCE onwards. In Hebrew and Aramaic, this sign designates two sibilant consonants – Shin and Sin. The early pronunciation of Sin is unknown, but at a certain phase of its evolution it became similar to that of Samekh (In modern South-Arabic languages, the pronunciation of Sin is still distinguished from that of both Shin and Samekh). In Hebrew, Sin is distinguished from Shin by a dot above its left "arm" , Shin having the dot above its right "arm".

In the cursive Nabataean script, the sign continued to change its form. First, the left-hand downstroke became vertical and increased in length , and later curved at the bottom to the left in the direction of writing. In rapid writing, the right-hand strokes were drawn continuously, without lifting the writing implement from the writing surface . In the course of time, the letter became smaller and more curved , and this is its form in the Arabic script. When not joined to the following letter, it terminates in a large, concave curved stroke س .

In Arabic, as in Hebrew and Aramaic, this sign designates two consonants – Shin and Sin, the Shin being surmounted by three dots ش. Both can join the immediately preceding and following letters. In certain styles of the Arabic script, the two small curves became a long line, while the dots became a small inflection resembling an acute accent .

ت ث *Ta:', Ṯa:'*

T

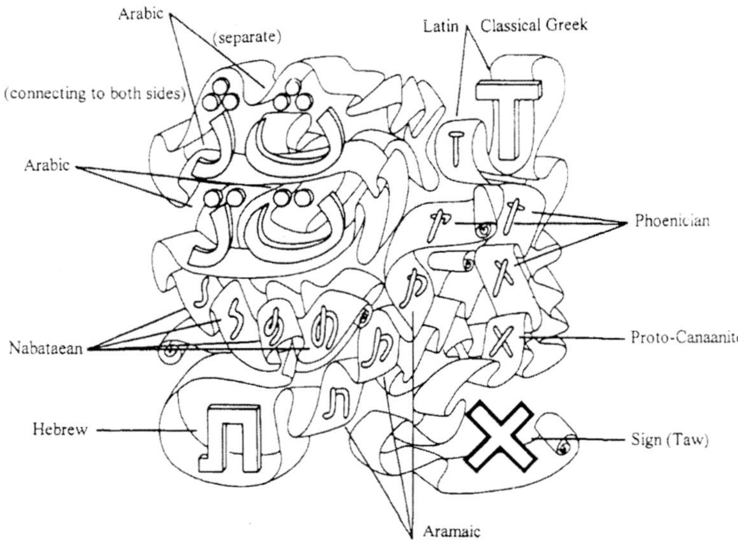

ת *Taw*

The Hebrew alphabet retained the ancient order of the letters. The last letter in the Hebrew alphabet is called Taw (the Hebrew word for '**sign**'). Its early form consisted of two crossed strokes + ×. This form already appears in inscriptions dating from about the 19th century BCE recently discovered at Wadi el-Hol in Egypt. This is the earliest evidence of the so-called Proto-Canaanite script; however, although most of the signs seem clear enough, the language has not yet been identified.

In the Greek script, the letter stands on one stroke, while the other has moved upwards + > ϯ > T . This is the form adopted by the Latin script and its phonetic expression is the same in most of the languages using the Latin script, although it may sometimes be modified by the adjacent sounds, as in the English "th".

In the Phoenician script, the stroke running down to the left became very long in relation to the short stroke that runs

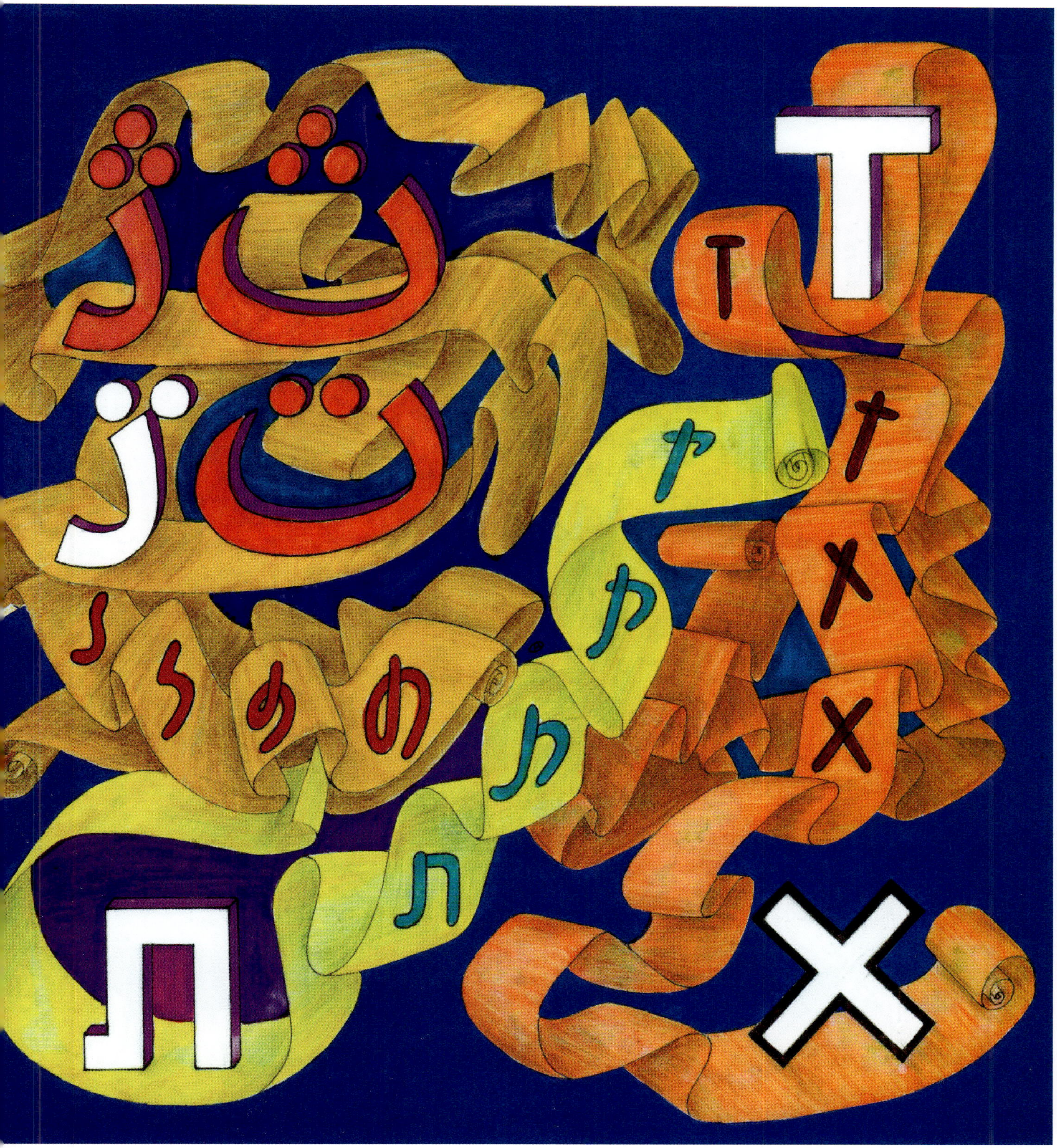

down to the right  . This is the form inherited by the Aramaic script. In the course of time, the crossed form was abandoned and instead, the short right-hand stroke emerged from the long one below its top and later curved downwards at its right extremity 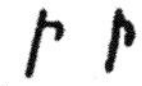 . This is the form of Taw in the Aramaic script in about the late 6th and early 5th centuries BCE. In the course of time, the right-hand stroke became longer while the left-hand stroke gradually shortened, curving to the left at the bottom  towards the 4th century BCE. This was the form of Taw when the local scripts, including the "Jewish" script, emerged from the cursive Aramaic script after the conquest of the Persian Empire by Alexander the Great.

In the Nabataean cursive script (and at a certain stage in the evolution of the letter in the "Jewish" script), a loop was created on the left-hand side of the letter. This resulted from drawing the left stroke before the right one; in rapid writing, the letter was drawn in one line without interruption, and the curved, lower end of the left stroke was drawn towards the beginning of the right stroke, creating a loop  . This loop gradually became smaller and higher  >  > until it completely disappeared, and the form of Taw became identical with that of Bet, Yod and Nun  .

In the Arabic script, two diacritical dots were added above the Ta:' تـ. However, in Arabic, this sign also designates the consonant /ṯ/ (as in the English "thing"). As mentioned above, in the ancient Canaanite inscriptions this consonant was designated by the pictogram of a composed bow, and its sign later came to designate Shin. In the South-Arabic and Ethiopic scripts /ṯ/ is designated by a special sign. However, the Nabataean version of the Aramaic script did not use a special sign for this consonant, and so the Arabic scribes added three diacritical points above Tha:' to distinguish it from Ta:'. Both letters join to the letters on either side, and when they do not join to the letter immediately following on the left, their form is a large, concave curve ت ث .

***

In addition to the calligraphic and formal scripts used for representative inscriptions and documents, such as memorial or dedicatory inscriptions or sacred scriptures, cursive script styles evolved in the Latin, Hebrew and Arabic scripts mainly as a result of rapid or spontaneous writing in ink. Different script styles evolved in different periods and in different places. Manuscripts written in cursive script styles are usually difficult to read without special training. The cursive script styles in use today are relatively new and their forms have been more or less fixed since they came to be used in printing. As against the great changes occurring in the cursive scripts, the basic forms of the letters in the representative, classical scripts have changed very little, and even an untrained modern eye may recognize Hebrew, Roman or Arabic letters in ancient inscriptions and manuscripts dating from 1500-2000 years ago.

Selected Bibliography:

Cross, Frank Moore, 'Newly Found Inscriptions in Old Canaanite and Early Phoenician Scripts', *Bulletin of the American School of Oriental Research* 238 (1980), pp. 1-20.

Darnell, John Coleman, *Theban Desert Road Survey in the Egyptian Western*, Oriental Institute of the University of Chicago Publications (Chicago, 2002).

Diringer, David, *The Alphabet: A Key to the History of Mankind* (London 1948); idem, *The Story of the Aleph-Beth* (New York-London 1960); idem, *A History of the Alphabet* (Henley-on-Thames, 1983).

Naveh, Joseph, *Early History of the Alphabet: An Introduction to west Semitic Epigraphy and Paleography* (Leiden 1982); idem, *Origins of the Alphabets*, Introduction to Archeology (Jerusalem, 1994).

Viers, Rina (Ed.), Des signes pictographiques a l'alphabet, Actes du colloque international, Beaulieu-sur-Mer 1996 (Arthala-Association Alphabets, 2000).

Sass, Benjamin, On the Origin and Early History of Northwest Semitic, South Semitic and Greek Alphabets, *Studia Alphabetica*, (Freiburg-Goettingen 1991).

Born and residing in Jerusalem, Dr. Ada Yardeni is a graduate of the Bezalel School of Art, where she received a diploma in graphic arts and calligraphy, and of the Hebrew University of Jerusalem, where she earned a Ph.D. in ancient Semitic languages, palaeography and epigraphy. She specializes in the study of Hebrew and Aramaic scripts and in the decipherment and interpretation of ancient inscriptions and documents, including Hebrew, Aramaic and Nabataean documentary texts from the Judean Desert and the Aramaic documents from Elephantine. She has designed a number of typefaces, one of which bears her name.
Among her publications are: *The Book of Hebrew Script* (Jerusalem 1997); *Textbook of Aramaic, Hebrew and Nabataean Documentary Texts from the Judean Desert and Related Material* (Jerusalem 2000); (Together with B. Porten:) *Textbook of Aramaic Documents from Ancient Egypt*, vols. I-IV (1986-1999); (Together with Hannah M. Cotton:), Aramaic, Hebrew and Greek Documentary Texts from Nahal Hever and Other Sites, *DJD* XXVII (Oxford 1997); (Together with Y. Yadin, J.C. Greenfield, and B. Levine:) *The Documents from the Bar-Kokhba Period in the Cave of Letters* (Jerusalem 2002); and some thirty scientific articles on various palaeographical and epigraphical issues.